Co/7381/£1.50

THE GOZO AFFAIR

THE GOZO AFFAIR
Kay King

Abelard-Schuman
London

I.S.B.N. 0 200 71870 3

LONDON
Abelard-Schuman Limited
8 King Street W.C.2.

Made and Printed by
The Garden City Press Limited
Letchworth, Hertfordshire
SG6 1JS

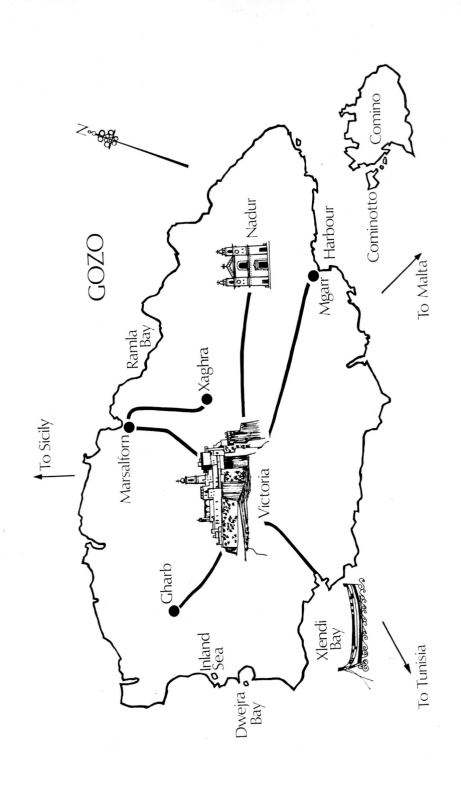

CHAPTER ONE

The file of cars waiting in a long line outside the entrance to the ferry at Marfa began to inch forward towards the gate. Mike noticed his father hadn't even bothered to switch on the ignition. He nudged him. 'They're moving,' he said encouragingly. His father took no notice but went on staring in an abstracted way at the boot of the car in front of them. Mike watched it edge forward another yard or two. 'I think we're moving,' he said again, more hopefully than truthfully. As the gap increased to about five yards Mike sat on the edge of his seat, his body tense, hoping that the sight of someone ready for action might galvanize his father into some sort of activity—but it was a wasted effort. Robert sat there, immobile.

At last the car behind them revved up and honked impatiently and Mike twisted round and made a sympathetic face at the driver. He shrugged his shoulders and jerked his head sideways at Robert. He didn't want anyone to think it was anything to do with him.

'Mike.' Robert's voice was as patient and passionless as ever. 'You might just as well calm down. I've no intention of moving until there's somewhere to move to.'

Within a few minutes, however, the Cortina in front shot forward on to the quay and it was the Bennets' turn at last. Robert switched on, slid the car quietly and efficiently into gear and moved up to the ticketman, whose creased brown face wrinkled up into a

5

welcoming smile as he looked at Mike. 'First time to Gozo?' he asked, fumbling for change in his brown leather satchel.

Mike grinned back at him but before he could say a word Robert smiled briefly and unencouragingly at the man, put his foot down on the accelerator and glided off. Mike scowled at his father and leaned out of the window and waved energetically at the ticket-man.

Two men in shorts and singlets beckoned them forward and Robert swung the car round expertly in a wide arc and bumped over the iron ridge where the car deck of the *Calypsoland* actually met the jetty. He brought the car to a halt, got out and carefully locked the door while Mike hopped out quickly and slammed it just hard enough to make his father wince. Together they made their way up the narrow staircase and came out on the scruffy top deck.

It was still very early—not yet half-past seven—but the air was already warm and the sunlight was brilliant. Mike went straight over to the side of the ship and looked down at the water. Small waves rippled round the boat, broke, reformed and then lazily made their way to the shore. Mike gazed at the grey island, clearly visible from the shore. It was bare and deserted, not a boat swung at anchor there, nothing moved. 'That's not Gozo, is it?' he asked, a note of disappointment in his voice.

'No. It's Comino.' Robert crackled his newspaper and turned over a page without bothering to look up.

'It'll be busy enough later in the season.' Mike swung round and saw a short, plump, smooth-faced man standing behind him. He beamed at Michael and thrust out a hand. 'My name is Carlo Caldena,' he said, 'and yours is . . .'

Robert got to his feet. 'My dear Carlo,' he said. 'I

6

didn't know you were on board. Let me introduce my son Michael.'

Caldena put out his hand and Mike thrust his out and gripped it. Instead of the podgy squeeze he'd vaguely expected, Caldena had a remarkably strong grip. 'How do you do?' Mike murmured politely.

'How do you feel?' asked Caldena. 'The night-flight's not much fun, is it?'

'It's not bad.' Actually Mike was beginning to feel quite lively. He'd felt really exhausted by the time they had touched down at Malta but the drive to the ferry had woken him up. ' You weren't on the flight, were you?' he asked.

'No, no. I've just come over from Sicily.' Caldena took out a handkerchief and rubbed it over his face. 'It's getting hot already, isn't it?'

'Signor Caldena,' Robert explained to Mike, 'is probably Gozo's longest weekend visitor. He came here more than a year ago on a flying visit, bought a house and has only been back once or twice since. He still insists, however, that he's not stopping.'

Caldena folded his handkerchief neatly and put it away, his white teeth glistening in his tanned face. 'It's my sixth visit home, Robert,' he said. 'You are joking again.' Joking *again*, thought Mike. He'd never even heard his father making anything resembling a joke before. 'Somehow,' Caldena went on, 'Gozo has become more of a home to me than Palermo is. It's lucky, I suppose, that I'm able to work almost any-where.'

Suddenly there was the roar of an engine and Mike looked up. 'The milk lorry,' said Robert. 'Good, we'll be off soon.'

Mike hung over the rails and watched the lorry zooming through the iron gates and hurtling down to the end of the quay as if to throw itself off. However,

7

the driver stamped hard on the brakes at the last moment and then stuck his head out of the cab. A number of men, their feet bare and their trouser legs rolled up, rushed down the jetty after it, all talking, all waving their arms about and all apparently giving contrary instructions.

The driver took no notice of any of them. He expertly manoeuvred the big tanker backwards and forwards in a series of little spurts and jolts until he was facing the right way and then, with another surge of power, he rolled over the iron plates and bucketed on to the ship. The *Calypsoland* shuddered violently, momentarily lurched on to one side and then gradually stopped her nervous quivering and settled down once again.

There was a lot more shouting and signalling and finally the rusty old iron chain and the rope hawsers were cast off. Then the engine, throbbing loudly, made a great effort and the ship inched away from the jetty and made her way out into the deeper water towards Comino.

Mike turned round. His father and Caldena had moved away, still talking. Mike eyed them. The contrast, he thought, was almost ludicrous. There was his father, tall, lean and slightly stooped, while Caldena, short and round though he was, positively glowed with vitality. Unlike Robert, who was dressed in shapeless old grey flannels and a faded blue shirt, Caldena was wearing a dark grey suit with a dazzlingly white shirt and a sombre tie. Neither of them glanced his way and so he turned back just in time to see Comino slide past.

Its bulk had been hiding another island; an island which rose like a greyish-brown fort out of the blue and silver sea that lapped it like a moat; an island which changed its shape and form second by second.

The sheer-sided cliffs developed bays and inlets, the bare earth became green and then, quite suddenly, buildings looking just like square building-blocks popped up. A long grey structure revealed itself as a church apparently perched high on a cliff-top, and then as Mike stared at it, it retreated and he could clearly see land in front of it. Trees came into focus, tiny cubes grew into houses, the toy boats littering the moat became fishing boats in a port and the port itself, originally the merest crack in the fortress, turned out to be a wide and generous bay. The match-box cars became life-sized, the vague splotches of colour were transformed into trees and plants and flowers, and, as the *Calypsoland* honked her way to the jetty, the huddle of ants on the quay became people waving enthusiastically at the boat.

Mike swung round excitedly but his father and Caldena had moved over to the staircase. He hurried across. 'It looks fabulous,' he began, but his father went on talking to Caldena. 'No,' he was saying, 'I really don't think I could possibly spare the time.'

'Don't make up your mind immediately, Robert,' Caldena said. 'Think it over.' He hovered, one foot on the top rung. 'If you should want any more information,' he said, 'I shall not be at home this evening but I shall certainly be at the Duke round about nine.'

Robert ran his hand over his chin thoughtfully. 'I really don't think I'm likely to change my mind,' he said, 'but I will give you a definite answer soon.' He turned round and gazed blankly at Mike for a second as if he couldn't quite remember who he was. 'Ah, Mike, yes. We're here.' He gripped Mike's elbow. 'Come along. We'll go down to the car. Perhaps it will be fairly clear down there by now.'

It was a vain hope. All was noise and confusion down below as people sat in their cars revving them up for all the world as if they were waiting for the start of a Grand Prix instead of for the departure of the milk lorry. Unperturbed by the racket that was going on all around him, the driver slowly clambered into his cab, switched on, switched off, fumbled for a cigarette and a light, had a last word with his friends and switched on again. Finally he threw the lorry into gear and drove rapidly on to the quay so that the ship lurched and shuddered alarmingly, and then he shot off out of sight. Robert sat there quietly waiting until it was his turn to roll over the iron plates, through the gates and out into Mgarr.

As Robert sped through the town Mike poked his head out of the window but he only got the most fleeting impression of square, flat-topped houses, of brown faces and bare arms and legs, of bright pink trees, of kids in school uniform, of red telephone boxes—red telephone boxes!

'Red telephone boxes!' he shouted to his father. Fancy seeing something so familiar in the middle of the Mediterranean!

'Yes.' Robert concentrated on passing a truck painted with hearts and flowers and various religious texts that was trundling along, swerving from one side of the road to the other. Then he drove even more carefully past a donkey and cart. The donkey was trotting along quite happily, a battered straw hat on its head and a large blanket slung beneath its stomach, while the driver, comfortably sprawled in the cart with one leg cocked over the side, nodded amiably to Mike, who immediately swung round and gave him a vigorous wave back.

'Really, Mike,' said Robert mildly.

There was a sudden glimpse of a huge fortress-like rock rearing high above the flat land below and then, as they shot round a corner, Robert took a turning to the right. Mike twisted his head as they passed a signpost. 'Xaghra,' it said. 'Exagra,' he repeated. 'We're nearly there, then.'

'Shara,' Robert corrected him. 'Pronunciation's odd here. "X" is "Sh." You'll get used to it.' He glanced in his mirror and moved in towards the safety of the verge as a battered old American car overtook them, hooting loudly all of the time and raising great puffs of fine grey dust.

Mike looked back the way they had come. They had been climbing ever since they took the Xaghra road and now, down below, he could see a huge domed church, while beneath him was the sea again, the boats once more shrunk to match-box size. 'What's the Duke?' he asked suddenly.

'The Duke. Oh, the Duke of Edinburgh. It's a hotel, pub, club—anything you want it to be really,' said Robert. 'If you get a bit lost at first, that's the place to go. There'll always be someone there who'll help. Everyone goes there.' He kept his eyes fixed on the road.

'A kind of mini-Piccadilly Circus,' said Mike.

Robert swerved to avoid a dog that was ambling across the road. 'Piccadilly Circus?'

'If you wait long enough everyone goes past,' said Mike.

'Not a very good analogy,' said Robert.

'Oh,' said Mike.

They entered quite a large village and reached a wide square and then turned down a road squashed to almost nothing by the great bulk of a church that almost filled one side of it. Robert slowed down. The narrow street was packed with a small army of young uniformed children, all dragging along satchels and cases. They grinned and waved and called out 'Hallo' and 'Good morning' and Mike felt faintly regal as he smiled and nodded back.

Robert eased his way through them and almost immediately pulled up outside a stone house, its front door faded but with its large key-hole and brass knocker brightly shining. As they got out of the car and Robert fumbled in his pocket for the key, the door swung open.

Robert's housekeeper, Anita, stood there smiling at them, her neatly coiled hair gleaming and her dark brown eyes warm and friendly. As Mike smiled back she put her hand on his shoulder and drew him in.

'Hallo, Anita,' said Robert briskly. 'This is Mike. I should think he's starving by now.'

She nodded understandingly. 'I have breakfast ready for you both,' she said. She took a good look at Mike. 'You are very like your photograph,' she said. 'but you are older than I thought.'

Mike looked staggered and his father confused. Whoever would have thought Robert kept an old picture of him!

'Er—well, yes, Mike. Your room is upstairs at the end of the passage facing you. The bathroom's next door. Have a quick wash and come down for breakfast. You can have a bath and a rest later on.'

For a moment Mike thought of protesting. He wasn't going to have his father ordering him around like a kid all through his holiday. Still, he couldn't actually be bothered to argue now, not just at this moment. He was too hungry for that.

He ran up to his room, opened the window and stepped out on to the small balcony and gazed across at the green valley. It seemed very cool and quiet. He went into the bathroom and splashed a token amount of water on his face and bounded down the stairs again. Anita was waiting for him. She pointed down the hall. 'That leads to the terrace,' she said. 'Your father usually has his breakfast out there.'

Mike wandered out into the shady, tiled yard. His father was already sitting at the table, his neatly folded newspaper by his side. A large pot of coffee together with toast and a bowl of fruit was on the table and Mike gave a sigh of pure satisfaction and sat down as Anita appeared with two plates of scrambled eggs.

He drank his coffee slowly and looked at the shining cutlery and the marble-topped table and the gleaming tiles at his feet and then he stared round at the golden-brown walls with vines clambering up them. He gave a quick glance at his father who was placidly eating breakfast and he thought of his mother. 'It'll mean pigging it for a bit, Mike,' she had said when telling him he had to stay with his father, 'but we'll make up for it later.'

As if he could read Mike's thoughts, Robert put down his newspaper and looked directly at him. 'It's hardly Knightsbridge,' he said, a trifle defensively, 'but it suits me.'

Mike thought of saying 'It suits me too,' but somehow it would have seemed a bit patronizing, especially to someone he hardly knew. So he concentrated on his eggs for a bit. 'Signor Caldena seems all right. What does he do?' he said at last.

Robert leaned back and placed his fingertips together and stared hard at them. 'Well,' he said at last, 'he's an amateur historian—a remarkably good one, as a matter of fact. He's by way of being an expert on maps.'

Crikey! He must be marvellous, Mike thought to himself. His father, as a professional, despised people who merely dabbled in things.

'Does he do anything else or is he just loaded?'

'Loaded?' Robert was puzzled.

'With loot—lolly—you know, money.'

Robert frowned. 'Then why not say so,' he said irritably. 'As a matter of fact he writes film scripts.'

Mike's face lit up. 'The flickers!' he exclaimed, hardly noticing the scrambled egg that fell from his fork.

A look of distaste crossed Robert's face. 'Yes,' he said shortly and lapsed into silence. By the time he'd had another cup of coffee, however, he'd recovered himself enough to say, 'As a matter of fact Carlo was suggesting that I might give his company my professional advice. They intend to make a film—an historical epic, he called it—on Malta and he thought I might be interested.'

'Sensational!' Mike was so excited he could hardly keep still.

'I dare say it will be,' Robert said drily.

'What have you got to do?' Mike leaned forward eagerly, his elbows on the table.

'I *have* to do nothing.' Robert's voice was cold. 'And it's unlikely I shall.'

Mike was knocked out by this. He ran his fingers through his thick reddish hair so that tufts were left standing like a cock's comb. 'You can't let a chance like that go. It could be . . .'

'It could be a number of things. The one certainty is that it will be a distraction. I'm already behind on my own work.'

'But you can't . . .' Mike began despairingly.

Robert turned a page of his newspaper over. 'I shall think it over,' he said pointedly, 'on my own.'

Mike sat there, his mouth open, his chin resting in the palms of his hands, and gazed at his father. He must be mad, he thought. No one in his right mind would turn down a chance to work in films. Still, he decided pityingly, his father probably still thought the flickers were silent. He probably thought writing a script meant writing the captions that used to be flashed on underneath. Mike shook his head. Robert just didn't know what ticked these days. That's what came of burying yourself in the fifteenth century. After a time you probably began to think you were in it.

He reached for a peach and gazed round the garden. It was nothing like an English one. He hardly recognized any of the trees that were glowing with near-fluorescent flowers. Through them he could catch glimpses of the green valley and on the far side of it, a row of houses strung like amber beads across a honey-coloured ridge.

'Your mother well?' Robert's polite, cool voice cut across his thoughts.

'Um—yep—she's fine. Busy with the new shows though. She's doing Paris now and then it's Rome. Still, you know that, don't you, otherwise I wouldn't be . . .'

'Yes.' Robert's unspoken comment that she was too busy with her own career to look after her son hung unspoken in the air. Not that he could talk, Mike thought resentfully. How often had he seen his father in the past five years? Six or seven times perhaps and only then when Robert had had to come to England to see his publisher or something.

'And how long . . .?'

'I think she's hoping I can stay until September,' Mike said and was infuriated to see a look of annoyance cross Robert's face. 'It's not only the shows, you see,' he said quickly. 'There's her column and she's writing a book about the rag trade too.'

Robert sat back, an astounded look on his face. 'A

book! But that's absurd! Not that your mother isn't a
competent journalist, but she surely hasn't the
capacity . . .'

'She's got a staggering advance,' said Mike. 'It's
colossal. Her publisher's convinced she'll make a
bomb.'

Robert pulled himself together. 'Really?' he
sounded cool enough but Mike could tell he was
furious, absolutely seething inside. 'Now what about
that bath? You'll probably need a sleep. I'll be in my
study if you want anything. I must get on.'

Mike grinned to himself as his father got up. Serve
him right, he thought. He knew that telling him about
the book would make him mad, but why shouldn't he
have been told? After all, he'd have heard about it
sooner or later. Quite suddenly he realized he was
feeling hot and sticky. The idea of a bath appealed.
He would flop down and read afterwards.

It was the sound of voices that woke him. He
struggled up out of sleep, shoved on some clothes and
went out to the balcony and leaned over. His father, a
polite, tight smile on his face, was sitting at a table
together with a huge man whose grey-streaked brown
hair hung over his collar and fell constantly in his eyes
so that he was forced to shake his head like a great
cart-horse every two or three minutes. The large man
was clearly excited about something and kept crashing
his massive fist down on the table.

'Haven't listened to a word I've said . . . she's been
out of action for weeks . . . laid up . . . thought I'd got
the best advice . . .' Poor guy, Mike thought. It
sounded as if his wife was in hospital. 'Had a refit
only last year . . .' What on earth could be wrong with
her? 'And now we need a new set of sails.' Mike

laughed aloud. He was carrying on about a boat, not a woman.

Robert looked up. 'Mike,' he said, a note of relief in his voice. 'Come down and meet some friends of mine.'

Mike rushed down the stairs and hurtled into the yard and almost fell over a girl who was sitting on the ground, her long brown legs stretched out in front of her. She tossed her fair hair out of her eyes and smiled up at him.

'James,' Robert began, but the massive man heaved himself out of his chair and went over to Mike and thumped him heavily on his back.

'I know,' he boomed. 'You're Mike. I'm James Wellington and I always . . .'

'Put my foot in it,' intoned the girl, a bored look on her face. 'It's the only joke James knows.'

'Saucy hussy!' said James severely, but he gave her a friendly tap on her back. 'She's my niece, Jenny. Look at her,' he went on. 'I've told her before about coming out half-naked. Doesn't take any notice of me though.'

Mike looked over at her. She was wearing denim shorts and a thin shirt. He couldn't see what James was on about.

'That's enough, James,' she said firmly. 'It's no good doing the heavy-uncle act just because you're out visiting. It doesn't fool anyone.'

'She's getting above herself these days,' said James in a pleased voice. Clearly, the more she answered him back the more he liked it. Robert, however, had a very disapproving look on his face. James turned back to Mike. 'Pity you're not up to a swim though. Just thought we'd call in and see.'

'But I . . .'

'I said I thought you'd probably be too tired, Mike,'

said Robert quickly. 'That night-flight takes more out of you than you realize.'

'But . . .'

'You're not missing much,' Jenny said, examining the sole of her bare foot. 'It'll be too crowded by now. Really it was all James's idea. He's been restless ever since his boat went into dock. He just prowls around all day long.'

'Absolute balderdash!' exclaimed James.

Jenny got to her feet. 'Why not come down tomorrow? We'll pick you up in the morning. That all right, James? Good, then let's travel. We've taken up too much of Robert's time already.' James stood there hesitantly and she turned and grasped his arm and tugged at him. 'Home, James,' she said. She looked across at Robert. 'Sorry about this,' she said. 'He always seems to think it's time for tea or coffee or something. It's a bad habit of his but I'm trying to break him of it.'

'Oh, of course . . . I simply wasn't thinking. You must stay. Do have a drink.' Robert, much to Mike's amusement, was flustered at having been caught wanting. 'I really wasn't thinking . . .'

Jenny towed James to the door. She swivelled round on the doorstep and grinned at them, her bright blue eyes glittering with malicious pleasure. 'Now I've embarrassed you, Robert,' she said contritely. 'I *am* sorry.' But she winked at Mike as they drove away.

CHAPTER TWO

Mike had hardly finished his breakfast the following morning before there was a thump at the front door. He leapt up and threw it open and found Jenny leaning casually against the wall while James sat in his dirty Land-Rover with the engine ticking over.

'Ready?' she asked.

'Sure.' Mike was just going to slam the door when she thrust her foot in the crack.

'Where are your swimming things?'

'Swimming things?' he echoed stupidly.

'Swimming things,' she repeated. 'Just think, my dear Michael. We are living on an island. Islands are surrounded by sea. This is a hot climate. In hot climates . . .'

'Okay, okay, there's no need to spell it out. I get the point.' Much to his fury Mike could feel his face getting red. 'I forgot. Hang on. I won't be a moment.'

'Shove your trousers over your trunks,' she shouted after him as he leapt up the stairs two at a time, 'and bring a sweater just in case.'

James turned his weather-beaten face to Mike as they climbed into the Land-Rover together. 'Nagging you already, is she?' he rumbled as he released the brake. 'Take my advice, Mike. Put her in her place once and for all.'

'Just like James has,' said Jenny gravely. 'He's got me completely under his thumb.' She pushed a map into Mike's hands. 'Use this. It's easier if you know where you're going. This is where we are now.' As she leaned over him her long hair tickled his nose but he didn't like to push it out of the way. 'Look, we're going to Xlendi . . .'

'Spelt XL?' asked Mike.

'Very good, well done,' Her tone was mocking but she glanced at him approvingly. 'We're going to go through Victoria.'

Mike looked alternately at the map and at the view as they went down the same hill he had come up with his father the previous day. He had a slight feeling of triumph when they turned on to the Victoria road and he found he recognized it immediately. But as they swung into a bewildering set of twists and turns through narrow crowded streets he began to feel despondent.

'Cheer up, partner,' said Jenny. 'By the time you've done this half a dozen times it'll feel just like the King's Road.'

They left the houses behind and started down a long hill, swung round a corner and over a bridge and there, unexpectedly, a long way below them, was the sea again. Facing it was a straight line of low buildings and beyond those a squarish bay that actually seemed to embrace the bluest water Mike had ever seen. Sheer grey cliffs overhung one side and a high but gentler one, with a row of houses clinging to it, leaned over the other. Mike took a deep breath. 'Fabulous!' he breathed, and then it was gone again. The road wound its way down the hill and there were more quick, tantalizing flashes of blue before they rolled down the last few yards and came to rest by a low sea-wall.

Actually there wasn't much to Xlendi. There were a few low houses on one side and a line of boat-houses, some of which, open like caves, were used as shops. There was a small pink hotel and a new police station and that was it. The walk along the front was perhaps three or four yards wide and fifty or so long. Mike could now see that the houses on the cliff were reached by a very steep road that ran parallel to the right-hand arm of the bay. Fishing-boats, painted in bold primary colours, wide-open eyes decorating their prows, bobbed up and down in the water together with a number of other craft. A couple of yachts were anchored some way out, while on the horizon a large tanker trundled past. That was all there was but for Mike it had an extraordinary air of unreality as though it was a painted backdrop.

'Come on.' Jenny got out and strode some way along the front before realizing she was on her own. Mike had halted to look at some old ladies who were sitting in the shade making lace while James had stopped to inspect the engine of the Land-Rover. 'Come on,' she said again, going back and grabbing his arm. 'Look, see those rocks. That's where we usually swim from. You go and dabble your toes or something while I go up to the house.'

'What for?' asked Mike idly.

Jenny hesitated for a moment and then her face went pink. Suddenly she laughed. 'My swimming things,' she said. 'I forgot them.'

Mike walked round the bay to the rocks she had pointed out and found a flat spot where a low concrete bench had been erected. He slowly took off his trousers and shirt and stood looking at the water for a moment or two before he sat down in the sun.

There weren't many people about. A couple of dogs chased each other around, a car or two went up the hill, a few children splashed about in the shallow water and the boats rocked rhythmically up and down. Mike sat there, feeling utterly contented. Suddenly he became aware of a boy of about his own age standing close by and he looked up. The boy flashed a brilliant smile at him. 'Freddie,' he said, holding out his hand, 'Freddie Contelli.'

Feeling quite ridiculous, Mike got up and shook it. 'I'm Mike,' he said, 'Michael Bennet.' Then, unable to think of anything else to do, he sat down again. The boy regarded him steadily. Mike sat there feeling even more ridiculous. What on earth was he expected to do? 'Do sit down,' he said desperately. The boy grinned and collapsed on to the rock while Mike sighed with relief at having hit the right note. There was a long silence. 'Do you live here?' Mike asked at last.

Freddie shook his dark head. 'Not now. We have a house here in the summer but now we live in Victoria. You live with your father in Xaghra?'

'Yes.' Mike was surprised that Freddie should know who his father was.

'Ah!' Freddie fell silent again.

'Do you go to school?'

Freddie nodded solemnly. 'Every day.' Then he brightened up. 'Today, though, is a holiday, and so is tomorrow. Do you go to school?'

'Yes.' Somehow Mike felt he couldn't go on with this conversation any longer. He had to break it up. He glanced at Freddie, who was wearing swimming trunks too. 'Race you to that boat,' he said. And then seeing Freddie poised on the edge of the rock, he dived in. He swam on his own at a tremendous rate, using the powerful rhythmic crawl he'd been taught. Then, quite suddenly, he was overtaken by Freddie, who dog-paddled past at a furious rate so that when Mike still had several yards to go Freddie was already hanging on to the mooring rope, twisting idly round and round in the water.

'You swim very well.' There was no doubt that the

note of admiration in Freddie's voice was absolutely genuine.

Mike was amazed. 'Style's not everything,' he said as they swam back slowly side by side and heaved themselves out of the water to sit on the slab.

An older boy, his black curly hair sticking out wildly in all directions, trotted towards them. He was wearing old jeans and a tee-shirt with 'Manchester United' stencilled across it. Freddie jumped up. 'This is Tony Contelli,' he announced. 'He is my cousin.'

Once again Mike leapt to his feet, introduced himself and invited Tony to share the seat. At least there was no need to make conversation. Tony launched into one straight away.

'I am for them.' He jabbed his finger at his tee-shirt. 'Best in the world.' Mike nodded and tried to look enthusiastic. 'You have seen them? You are a fan?'

Mike confessed that he hadn't actually seen them and that he couldn't honestly call himself a fan. 'Who do you support then? Chelsea? Pah! They are no good, just sometimes lucky. Liverpool? Now they are better but not always as good as they should be. Sometimes they play only for themselves and not for each other.'

Tony, carried away with the excitement of having another fan to talk to, waved his arms about as he poured out words and jumped up and down over and over again to demonstrate some intricate point or other. Most of the time Mike hadn't the faintest idea of what he was on about, but he managed to keep an interested smile on his face and nodded intelligently whenever Tony paused for breath. 'And so,' Tony shouted, 'if Georgie Best went to Stoke and Heighway played for Sheffield then all would be better for the game but not for those others left behind.' He shot a quick look at Mike. 'Who then,' he demanded, 'do you support?'

'Er—' Actually Mike wasn't interested at all but he didn't like to disappoint Tony. 'Er—actually . . .' He rummaged around in his mind. What other teams were there? 'Um—Crystal Palace,' he said weakly, 'and . . . York,' he added for good measure.

Tony fell silent, an incredulous look on his face. 'Crystal Palace and York!' he said at last. 'Crystal Palace and York! Why do you support those? They are no good. See where they are in the league. Crystal Palace will go down and York will never go up. They are finished . . .'

'They've got plans for next season,' said Mike hastily. 'You'll see. It'll be a real turn up. You just wait!'

'Ah!' Tony regarded him thoughtfully. 'What do you know?'

Mike shook his head. 'Can't actually say,' he said, more or less truthfully, 'but believe me, you'll be hearing a lot about them.'

Tony nodded comprehendingly at him. 'Aha!' he said. 'Then we must say mum's the word.'

'That's absolutely right,' agreed Mike gratefully. 'Mum's the word.'

At last Tony clambered to his feet again and ran up and down on the spot for a moment or two before trotting off, arms held high and pumping away like pistons.

'Where's he going?' asked Mike.

'To practise,' said Freddie. 'He plays for Xewekia Tigers. He is very good, very fast, very energetic.'

'I bet.' Mike suddenly spotted Jenny in the distance. Tony, still trotting, chest out and back straight, circled her several times, obviously talking all the while, and disappeared round the corner while Jenny, now wearing a bikini with a towelling coat over the top, sauntered over to them.

24

'Hallo, Freddie,' she said, and then she turned to Mike. 'What have you been saying to Tony? He seems to think you're a junior coach, a talent spotter and sports writer all rolled into one.'

'Mike did not say much.' said Freddie. 'He had no chance. You know Tony. He sleeps and thinks and dreams football. I think he will throw himself from Dwera if he does not become the greatest player in the world.'

'Dwera?'

'High cliffs,' explained Jenny, as she grabbed hold of her hair and skewered it up into a sort of a bun on the top of her head. 'It's near the Inland Sea.' She caught a glimpse of Mike's baffled expression. 'One bit of the island must have been volcanic,' she went on, 'and the Inland Sea is like a great lake surrounded by cliffs. In one corner there's a tunnel that leads straight out into deep water. Some people are mad about it but I hate it. It gives me the creeps.'

Freddie got up and stared down at her. 'The creeps?'

'Yes, it's spooky. You, know—it feels ghostly.'

'Ha! That is because you are a girl,' said Freddie arrogantly.

'Ha!' echoed Jenny, grabbing his ankle with one hand and giving him a little push. 'That's because you are a boy.' She suddenly let go and pushed harder. Freddie teetered on the edge of the rock, tried to keep his balance, his arms flailing about, before he fell into the sea. 'Come on,' she said to Mike. 'Let's go before he throws us in.'

Later, while they were all sprawled around drying off, a burly khaki-clad sunburned man strolled past and gave them a sort of half nod.

'Who's that?' asked Mike, lifting his head from his arms.

'Mr Roccia, the policeman,' answered Freddie, rolling over on to his back.

Mike looked round the placid bay. 'There can't be much for him to do here.'

'But yes!' Freddie jerked himself upright. He sounded almost indignant. 'We have a crime wave too. Last summer some boys from Malta stole from the cars—a transistor, I think, and sunglasses and other things—and then the police caught the smugglers . . .'

'Smugglers!' Somehow that sounded right on an island.

'Yes, they had clothes on board. Shirts and dresses and sweaters but they were captured when . . .'

'Clothes! Couldn't they do better than that?' Mike demanded.

Freddie wrinkled his brow. 'What else could they smuggle?'

'Well,' Mike propped himself on his elbows, 'gold or hash for instance.'

'Who would buy it?' said Freddie simply. 'People here are not rich enough. And anyway, what is hash?'

'Pot, grass, marihuana, reefers.' Freddie still looked uncomprehending. 'For smoking, you know.'

'But cigarettes are cheap on Gozo.'

'No, these are different cigarettes. They—er—well, if you smoke them you sort of forget your worries. You kind of enter another world,' said Mike vaguely. He'd never actually had any and he didn't know anyone personally who had. 'They're a kind of dope, a drug.'

'And they're no good, Freddie,' said Jenny sharply. 'Forget it.'

'Drugs!' Freddie's dark eyes widened. 'They are no good but Mike says that these are cigarettes. That is different.'

'No, it's not. It doesn't matter how you take the

stuff, whether it's smoked or injected or sniffed, it doesn't make any difference—it's still poison.'

'Come on now . . .' began Mike.

'They smuggle drugs in Sicily,' said Freddie. 'One of the Mafia has been caught and he is to have a trial. It was on the radio, but they say that he is to do with really bad drugs, that he is the centre of . . .'

'Listen, Freddie,' said Jenny. 'You remember that Englishman on Gozo who was so ill, don't you? He started by taking pot and then he went on to the hard stuff and you know what happened to him, don't you?'

'Yes,' said Freddie, his face serious. 'They had to take him away.'

'Ah, well,' said Mike. 'If he was on the hard stuff then that was different. He was probably addicted to it. Couldn't do without it.'

'Addicted.' Freddie practised the new word. 'Addicted.'

'Yes, an addict. He needed his dope.'

Freddie laughed. 'Then Tony's an addict. He's a football addict—a football doper.'

'Well, not exactly,' Mike began, and then he realized that since he could hardly explain the difference to himself he certainly couldn't explain it to Freddie. 'That's right,' he ended feebly. 'I suppose you might call him that.'

Freddie gave himself a quick rub and then hauled on his shorts. 'I must go,' he said, dragging his sweater over his head. 'It will soon be time for lunch.'

He was hardly out of earshot before Jenny sat up and glared at Mike, her blue eyes sparkling with anger. 'Well,' she snapped, 'and just how much pot have you smoked?'

Astonished by her attack, Mike sat up too. He clasped his arms around his knees. 'What's it got to do with you?'

27

'Well, have you?' she demanded fiercely.

'No.'

'Then stop shouting your mouth off about it.' She unpinned her hair so that it fell around her shoulders.

'What are you so worked up about? Everyone knows . . .'

'Everyone doesn't know. Even the experts don't agree . . .'

'What's got into you?' Mike was shouting now. 'What are you blowing your top for?'

'Calm down.' Jenny gave him a cool little smile.

Mike was even more infuriated by this. 'Calm down! You as good as accuse me of being a pusher or something and then you tell me to calm down . . .'

'Don't be so stupid. I didn't do anything of the sort. But what I am saying is to drop the chat about drugs. They get on fine without it. I reckon we do enough harm here one way and another without dragging all that in.'

'Harm? What are you getting at?'

'It's tough on them. They see us with things they can't possibly hope to have,' Jenny muttered. 'It doesn't seem fair somehow. It makes me feel guilty.'

'So that's it.' Mike sounded triumphant now. 'So your conscience is pricking. That's what it's all about.'

Jenny shrugged. 'Sure, that's part of it.' She brushed the hair out of her eyes and looked directly at him. 'Please, Mike,' she said, 'just don't talk about drugs in a casual way as though it's like eating a bar of chocolate. Look at Freddie. His English is marvellous but he doesn't catch on to everything straight away, does he?'

'Oh, okay,' said Mike, mollified. 'I'll watch it.'

Jenny ran her fingers through her hair. 'How do you get on with your father?' she asked.

'All right. Why?'

28

'I just wondered. He's an odd guy, isn't he? I mean, he really does prefer his own company. He must have been furious when he heard you were coming out.'

Mike stiffened. 'Perhaps you know a little less about my family than you imagine,' he said coldly, his icy tone very like his father's.

'Now come off it, Mike,' said Jenny easily. 'No one has a private life on this island. It just isn't done. We all know your mother was too tied up with the new collections to bother about you . . .'

Mike's face went red. 'It wasn't like that!' he snapped.

'Wasn't it?' Jenny had an amused look on her face. 'How was it then?'

'My school had an outbreak of German measles and since it was pretty near the end of term anyway they just packed up early. And because my mother was just starting on the fashion shows she . . .'

'As I said, she . . .' Jenny stopped short as she caught a glimpse of Mike's outraged expression. 'Sorry, sorry,' she said pacifically, 'have it your way. Your school packed it in, your mother was busy and your father couldn't wait to see you. Now you can have a go at me. What do you want to know?'

'What you're doing here.'

'That's easy. My school went broke. It was a progressive one and they usually do. My parents are in South America on a United Nations thing and there really wasn't anywhere for me to go. Then James turned up. I think my mother twisted his arm actually because I'd hardly ever met him before. He was in the Navy for years and ever since he came out he's lived in the Mediterranean.'

'Is he rich then?'

'Rich?' Jenny looked blankly at him. 'Dunno. Shouldn't think so. I think he's done all right in the past though. He's chartered his boat from time to time—trips to Greece and Turkey and that sort of thing. Why do you ask?'

'I don't know. I just sort of wondered. There seem to be quite a lot of English people on the island and knowing how hard my father works I wondered how they all got by.'

'Most of them are sixpenny people,' said Jenny. 'By bringing their money here they save on income-tax. They only pay sixpence in the pound.'

'Do you think they're happy?'

She shrugged. 'Who knows? They just sort of pretend they're in a kind of hot, brown England and they go on having bridge clubs and bring-and-buy sales just as if they were in a Sussex village. Mind you, there are plenty of others. Some of them are really odd.' She suddenly jumped to her feet and waved. 'James is signalling,' she said. 'Lucky he hasn't got any flags or it would be in semaphore. Come on, pull yourself together, Mike, it's food.'

'Where?'

'Over at St Patrick's, the hotel. An omelette and salad, I should think.'

James went on shouting and waving until they were almost under his nose. 'Late again!' he exploded. 'You're always late! Look at that.' He shoved a limp and leathery omelette under their noses. 'It's ruined.'

Jenny, completely unperturbed by this, sat down. 'You do it every day,' she said. 'I keep telling you—wait until we get here before ordering.'

James swivelled round. 'Rosa,' he yelled, looking at a pretty girl who was sitting on a stool just inside the hotel. 'We'll start all over again.'

She slipped off her stool and came over and picked

up the plates. She paused for a moment and looked at Mike. 'You are very like your father,' she said.

Horrified, Mike stared at her back as she disappeared inside again. Surely he didn't. He couldn't have acquired that long mournful face and that thin colourless hair overnight.

'You're nothing like him,' said Jenny. 'She just thought she'd please you. Actually you're much more like your mother.'

'How do you know?' he asked.

'Pick up any paper or magazine these days,' said Jenny, 'and you're sure to see a picture of her laying down the law about fashion.'

Mike flushed. 'I guess it seems like that,' he said, 'but I reckon she really knows what she's talking about.'

'Maybe,' Jenny said noncommittally.

'I've seen her picture,' said James suddenly, helping himself to salad. 'Fine looking woman. Good lines.'

'Hope she never comes here,' said Jenny, 'otherwise he'll smash a bottle of champagne on her forehead and push her down the slipway.'

They chattered to each other all through lunch and then went on sitting there afterwards. It was really hot and it was just too much of an effort to move. James pulled a red-spotted handkerchief out of his pocket and covered his bulging neck with it. Then he took a thriller out of another and settled down to read.

Jenny suddenly waved at a fair-haired woman who was slowly wandering along the edge of the water. 'That's Sue,' she said approvingly. 'She's okay. You can tell her anything. She knows how to keep quiet. The others gossip all of the time, they thrive on it. Sometimes the island positively crackles with rumour. It builds up like static and then there's an explosion.'

The time shot past. James dropped off over his thriller but every few minutes he snorted loudly enough to wake himself up and then he read a few more pages before dropping off again and repeating the process.

Jenny chattered on, her face lively and glowing, and then quite suddenly it darkened and she fell silent. Mike twisted his head round and saw Caldena approaching. He came straight over to them. 'I thought,' he said, smiling at Mike, 'that I might find your father here.'

Mike shook his head. 'He told me he was working at home all day.'

'Really?' Caldena looked puzzled. 'How strange. I have just called at the house but he was not there.'

'Perhaps he didn't want to see you,' said Jenny coolly. There was a moment of silence and Caldena's smile slowly faded. 'Because of his work,' she continued smoothly.

'Yes.' Mike rushed in after his astonishment at her deliberate rudeness. 'I mean, even me, that is, anyone . . .'

'Of course.' Caldena's ready smile returned. 'I should have thought. I shall return and leave a note.' He executed a sort of bow in Jenny's direction and smiled apologetically at them both before leaving. Jenny watched him go, a contemptuous look on her face.

'What was all that about?' asked Mike curiously.

Jenny said nothing at first and then she shook her head. 'He's a dirty rotten low-down snake!'

'Snake! Snake!' James suddenly snorted himself awake again. 'Where?'

'Just slithering around the corner.'

James, puffy-eyed, squinted round. 'Can't see . . .- Oh! Caldena. Don't know what you've got against him, Jenny. He's harmless. Can't help looking smooth, you know. Comes natural to Italians.'

'Oh, don't be so silly.' She got up. 'Let's go to the house, Mike, and get a cold drink. I'm parched.' As they drifted along Mike brought Caldena up again but Jenny had clearly made up her mind she wasn't going to talk about him so after a bit he lapsed into silence as well.

Halfway up the hill she stopped and pushed open the door of a rather shabby house and they walked straight into the living-room. It was absolutely packed with things, with gadgets and electrical equipment, with books and records, papers and typewriters and even bits of boats.

Jenny got them both a drink and threw herself down on a divan. She laughed as she looked at Mike's astonished face. 'It's a jungle,' she said. 'but I can't do anything about it. It's James's room actually. He likes it like this.'

Mike surveyed it in silence. 'He *likes* it like this?' he repeated in an incredulous voice.

'Yep. Mind you, the boat's different. It's the only thing he really cares about. I should think it's the most efficient craft in the whole of the Mediterranean. With any luck it'll be ready on Thursday . . . I say, Mike, we'll be going over then, me and James and Mario, that is. Why don't you come too?'

'Mario?'

'Yes. He's another friend. Son of the doctor here.' She put her head on one side and listened intently. 'That's him now,' she said, her face lighting up. 'I'd know the Snorter anywhere.'

Mike listened too and heard a car crawling its way up the hill, wheezing and groaning loudly at the effort, and then it stopped outside the house. The door opened and a thin, dark, alert-looking face peered round. 'Anyone at home?'

Jenny jumped up, her fair hair bouncing up and

down on her shoulders. 'Mario!' she said warmly, and seized both his hands and dragged him in. 'Come in and meet Mike.'

Unsmilingly Mario thrust out his hand. 'Mario Timaldi,' he said.

Mike got up and gripped it. He knew the score now. 'I'm Mike,' he said. 'Mike Bennet.'

Mario looked at him, a curious expression on his face. 'I know,' he said. 'You support York.' The words were polite enough but the tone was almost contemptuous.

Mike reddened. 'Well, not exactly,' he said quickly, 'not . . .'

He stopped as a car roared up the hill and screeched to a halt. The car door was slammed and the door of the house was kicked open. James put his big head round it. 'So this is where you're hiding,' he shouted. 'Had to sweat all the way up here to find you. Thought you'd like a lift home. I'm going your way. Got to leave now though.'

'Perhaps I could catch a bus later,' said Mike hesitatingly.

'A bus! You're joking! They either run at the crack of dawn or not at all,' said Jenny. 'They certainly don't run in the late afternoon. No, you'd better go with James.'

James kicked a water ski so that it skidded noisily across the tiled floor. 'What's that doing there?' he demanded. 'Makes the place look a shambles.'

'That's where you dropped it.'

'Me?' James took off his jacket and slung it down on a chair. 'Course I didn't.' He turned to Mike again. 'Come on if you're coming then. I haven't got all day to waste. It's now or never.'

'Okay.' Mike hastily grabbed his things. 'It's now.'

34

CHAPTER THREE

Mike was standing on his balcony the following morning thinking to himself that he was just about ready for breakfast when there was a hammering at the front door. He leaned over and shouted down to Anita, who was busily laying the table on the terrace, 'I'll answer it,' and belted down the stairs and threw it open.

Jenny and Freddie stood there supporting three very old bicycles between them. 'Fancy a trip round the island?' asked Jenny.

Mike looked doubtfully at the bikes. None of them looked in a very good condition. 'On those?'

'Sure!' Jenny slapped her hand on the saddle of one of them and it nose-dived towards the crossbar. 'That's yours.'

Freddie forced the saddle back into position. 'It is the best one.'

'Where did you dig them up?' Mike tested the handlebars and frowned as they wobbled easily from side to side.

'They are my cousin's,' Freddie explained proudly. 'I borrowed them from him.'

'Are you coming or aren't you?' asked Jenny, sitting on hers and resting the tip of one foot on the ground.

'Why not?' Mike grabbed hold of his bike and cocked one leg over the crossbar. 'Wait a minute though. Swimming things.' He got off and raced indoors again and returned a couple of minutes later with his duffle bag slung over one shoulder. Anita followed him out into the street.

'What about your breakfast, Mike?'

He waved a backward hand as he pushed off. 'Don't want any, thanks.'

Jenny, who was still scooting along behind him, one foot on the pedal, turned round. 'We'll get some coffee later, Anita. I won't let him starve.' She made a determined effort and managed to get her leg over the bar at last and pedalled furiously in an effort to catch the others up.

Mike, who hadn't been on a bike for years, wobbled rather badly at first but as he swerved and rattled, bumped and bucketed and shook and bounced he began to feel he was astride some uncontrollable horse. The brakes, even when he jammed them full on, had almost no effect, and he was reduced to putting one foot on the ground as he reached corners and skidding round them. It became more and more exhilarating and, as the hill got steeper and steeper, he picked up speed and rushed down at breakneck pace.

'Yippee!' he yelled as he overtook Freddie. He waved a careless hand as he shot past him and almost ran into a herd of goats. More by luck than judgement he weaved his way safely in and out of them, but they turned reproachful faces as he pelted down the hill, their beards stirring in the little breeze he'd created.

All the way down, whenever he'd dared to lift his eyes, he'd seen flashes of blue appear and reappear and now the smell of the sea began to reach him. 'Slow down!' Freddie shouted as they came to a more built-up looking area. So Mike squeezed hard on his brakes without success and finally put down one foot and eventually managed to slither to a halt. He looked back. Freddie and Jenny were just flying round the last corner, Jenny's long hair streaming out like a banner. He waited until they had caught him up and then the three of them pedalled sedately into a sort of seaside village.

Freddie waved one arm. 'Marselforn,' he announced.

Mike glaned round the wide bay. Although it was still early it was already fairly busy. A number of small boats were buzzing round and round and a long way out someone was water skiing. Heads bobbed up and down in the water and a few people were sprawled in the sun. It wasn't exactly smart but it had an air of purpose and activity that appealed to him. 'It's all right, isn't it?' he said as he dismounted.

'What are you getting off for?' asked Jenny.

'Coffee,' said Mike. 'You said we'd have some.'

'But not yet. We've hardly started.' Jenny looked at him. 'Oh, all right, but don't let's take all day about it.'

She led the way to a small café and they sat under a faded umbrella. 'What's new, Guido?' she asked, as a small thin man brought them their drinks.

'I know,' said Freddie quickly. 'I heard on the radio this morning. Vesculdi has escaped. It was the most important news.'

'Vesculdi? Who's he?' Jenny frowned.

'I told you yesterday,' said Freddie reproachfully. 'He is the one in the Mafia who was to be tried. He was the centre of a drug ring. He arranged for it to come from Turkey to the Mediterranean.'

'The Mafia!' said Mike. 'I can hardly believe in it. It sounds like thirties stuff. You know, tentacles all over the world and that sort of thing.'

Jenny brushed a long strand of hair from her eyes. 'I know what you mean. Old George Raft flickers, ankle-length overcoats and wide-brimmed hats and machine-guns in violin cases and all that jazz. It isn't a joke though, Mike, it's for real. There's too much money involved in the racket for them to be able to afford a sense of humour.'

'That's right.' Freddie put his cup down. 'That is what they said on the radio. Vesculdi has no money because they have ...' He faltered, unsure of the best way to express himself. 'They have put his money on ice and so ...'

'Frozen it,' said Mike.

'But they say he will now try to get hold of the big amount of drugs believed to be on its way. I think they said a quarter of a million pounds.'

'A quarter of a million!' Mike whistled. 'Are you sure? It sounds a hell of a lot.'

'Yes,' said Freddie positively.

'Then I don't see the problem,' said Mike. 'Why don't they just search every boat in the Med? After all, it can't be that easy to hide. It must look like a mountain.'

Jenny leaned back in her chair. 'Of course it won't. It'll be pretty small, compressed into a package. You don't think they'd ship the raw stuff, do you? They do stage one before it leaves Turkey or wherever they've got it from, and the last bit where they turn it into heroin is done in Marseilles or Lyons.'

'But if they know it's carried out there,' argued Mike, ruffling his red hair as he spoke, 'why can't they stop it?'

'Do you realize how big Marseilles is? It isn't as if you need a big lab to process the stuff, a small room will do as long as you've got the know-how. I bet the police in France will be on their toes. Vesculdi's bound to make for there.'

'Do you think Sicily was a sort of staging post then?' asked Mike.

'It looks like it, doesn't it? With stuff worth that sort of money floating around I bet Vesculdi kept a very sharp eye on it indeed.' She glanced round at the clock. 'Let's push off. I'm late already.'

'It's a murderous business, isn't it?' said Mike, getting to his feet.

'Murder?' Freddie turned alarmed eyes on them. 'What do you mean?'

'Like I said yesterday,' said Jenny. 'Once you get hooked on something like heroin, you die. Not straight away, but in the end you die. You can't do without it. You just exist.'

'I see,' said Freddie thoughtfully. 'It is not good then.' He began to walk more briskly towards the bikes. 'Come,' he said to Mike. 'We have a lot to see.'

Mike looked at him warily. 'Have we?'

'It's none of my doing,' said Jenny hastily. 'Freddie fixed the programme, not me. I'm only coming as far as Victoria. After that, chum, you're on your own.'

'No, he is not,' said Freddie indignantly. 'He is with me.'

A thin cadaverous man hurried round the corner and almost fell over the bikes. Startled, he raised his pale blue eyes to Jenny and gave her a quick sharp nod of recognition before striding on. 'He's going to be late again,' Jenny remarked, watching him disappear round the corner.

'Late? Late for what? Who is he?'

'Edward Albion. He's late for everything,' said Jenny, picking up her machine, 'or nothing come to that. He's just got a thing about time. He can't bear to waste it.'

'So what does he do?'

'Nothing.'

Mike shook his head as he pedalled after them. People seemed to be quite mad on Gozo. Still, with any luck it might happen to him too and then he'd never have to leave it. He rose from the uncomfortable saddle and pressed on even harder until he caught the others up. Freddie eased up after a bit and pointed over to the right with one hand. 'Look,' he said 'that's the Citadel.'

There, rising almost sheer from the plain, was an immense natural rock, fortified at the top with buildings clustered inside the walls and crowned with an enormous, impressive church. A cross on the very top sparkled and glittered in the sunshine. 'It's fantastic!' said Mike. 'What is it?'

'A fortress,' said Freddie, a note of pride in his voice. 'Whenever the Turks swept in the people ran there for safety.'

'What did the Turks do? Give up and go home?'

'Once they got inside the Citadel. Nearly everybody was taken away to be slaves,' he explained.

'Chained to the galleys and all that?'

'Yes,' Jenny leaned on her bike and joined in too. 'It was the usual thing to do. A few escaped because they didn't believe the Citadel was safe enough and so they hid in caves instead . . .'

'And others got away because they were brave enough to escape by ropes.'

'Ropes!' Mike whistled softly as he looked at the sheer-sided cliff with its terrifying drop to the plain below. 'It'd take a lot of nerve to swing down there. I couldn't do it.'

Jenny shuddered. 'Nor me,' she said quietly.

'You might,' said Freddie. 'If the Turks were at your feet . . .'

'Heels,' said Mike.

'Heels, you might.'

'I guess so,' said Mike, twisting round to get a last look before they pushed on to Victoria. Jenny peeled off from them at the Xlendi crossroads. 'See you later,' she said cheerfully to Mike, 'if you survive, that is.' And Mike, already feeling a bit hot and saddle-sore, looked apprehensively at Freddie who seemed as fresh as when they had started out.

A couple of hours later he suddenly stopped and sat down under a tree. He pulled out his handkerchief and wiped it over his face. Freddie stopped, one leg resting on the ground, and looked back at him, a surprised expression on his face. 'Is something wrong?'

Mike turned a weary face to him. 'I'm flaked,' he groaned.

'Tired?' Freddie was amazed.

'That's right. Tired. Exhausted. All in.' Mike lay back in the shade and put his hands under his head.

'It is not the time to rest. We must go . . .'

Mike squinted up at him. 'Not me,' he said firmly.

Freddie twirled his pedal round and round. 'But we are near the sea. If we swim you will feel better.'

The sea. That sounded quite a good idea to Mike. He sat up again. 'How far?' he asked warily.

'Very close.' Freddie pointed down the hill. 'Five minutes only and it is all downhill.'

'Well—okay.' Mike clambered unenthusiastically on to his bike again and they wound their way down to the sea, rattled along a bumpy lane, dumped the machines at the end of it and turned into a wide bay where heavy rolling waves thumped heavily on to a vast coarse red sandy beach. Awkwardly, their feet sinking deep into the sand, they rushed along, ripping off their clothes as they went, and hurled themselves into the water.

By the time they came out Mike was feeling a lot more cheerful and he felt even better when Freddie went back to his bike and returned with a packet of sandwiches and fruit. Mike pointed round the coast. 'What's beyond those cliffs?'

'More cliffs,' Freddie said indistinctly, his mouth bulging. 'All Gozo is a cliff. You want to see?'

'No, no,' said Mike hastily. 'I like it here. Can't we stay?'

'No,' said Freddie firmly. 'We might not have the bikes again.'

Mike gave an inward sigh. He could see that Freddie had mapped out a programme and that nothing but total collapse would prevent him seeing it through. He lay back on the warm sand and closed his eyes. Maybe if he looked as if he was in an exhausted sleep Freddie would take pity on him but he was out of luck. A quarter of an hour later a determined Freddie shook him until he got up. Reluctantly he scrambled to his feet and floundered across the heavy sand and scowled at his hideous machine. 'It's all uphill,' he said. 'Maybe we'd better push.'

'But we can ride some of the way. We will only push when we must.' Freddie set off at quite a pace and Mike, groaning to himself, forced his aching legs to pedal after him. It hardly seemed possible that such a small island should take so long to cover and Freddie was indefatigable. They went through village after village, up one hill and down another, Freddie, always conscious of his role as guide, giving a running commentary the whole of the time.

Each time they set off again every journey was a new agony to Mike. Finally even Freddie seemed to realize that Mike was just about all in. He looked back at Mike's sweat-streaked face with some concern. 'Enough?' he asked, and Mike nodded, too tired even to utter a word.

Lips pressed tightly together he pedalled doggedly back to Xlendi behind Freddie, and though every muscle screamed for a rest he knew he simply dared not stop. If he did he'd just seize up. He'd never get going again. Even the final run down the hill was torture to him as he jerked and jolted and rattled along the final half mile of road. At last they slithered to a halt by the sea-wall and Freddie hopped off his bike and held Mike's for him while he slowly climbed off. 'All right?' he asked anxiously and Mike nodded weakly and managed a feeble smile. 'Okay then.' Freddie took hold of Mike's machine. 'I will return them to my cousin.'

Mike slumped against the wall. 'Do you want any help?' he mumbled.

'Do you?' Freddie stared anxiously at Mike's exhausted face.

Mike shook his head. 'I'm fine.'

'Well—all right. I must go. It is nearly time for the Band Club.'

Mike stumbled along the front and was on the point of collapsing into a cane chair when Jenny came out of the hotel. She grabbed his arm. 'You look all in. Don't sit here. Stagger up to the house with me. You can spread yourself there.' She clapped her floppy hat on to her head and grabbed her bag.

'I don't think I can make it,' muttered Mike.

'Of course you can,' she said briskly. 'Lean on me. I know what a Gozitan tour of the island's like.'

'It makes me feel so weedy,' groaned Mike as he hobbled along.

'You *are* a weed by their standards,' she said cheerfully, 'but don't let it get you down. They won't hold it against you. Where did you go?'

'Where didn't we go!' Mike limped slowly up the hill by her side. Suddenly Jenny took away her supporting arm and waved so that Mike came to a halt. A large shambling figure was peeping shyly round the corner of the house and then, seeing Jenny approaching, it capered towards her, arms outstretched, vague unintelligible grunts coming from its slobbering mouth. Mike was horrified. He almost cringed as it neared him.

The boy, his large head shaking uncontrollably from side to side, pranced clumsily round Jenny. 'Simon!' she said, real warmth in her voice. He gambolled round her again, his wide mouth dribbling with excitement. The overlarge head wobbled and nodded and the small eyes glittered. 'I haven't seen you for ages, Simon. Where have you been?'

The arms shot out in wide uncoordinated sweeps, the gutteral noises became more explosive and the vacant face screwed up into a grimace. 'Dw—Dw—Dw.'

'Dwera?' Jenny's voice was disapproving. 'You mustn't go there alone, Simon. It's much too far.'

The brilliance in the eyes dimmed. They suddenly filled and then gradually overflowed with tears which dripped down his face.

'I'm not cross with you, Simon,' said Jenny quickly. 'It's just that I miss you when you're not here.' The mouth immediately twisted back into a grin although the tears went on flowing down his face. She pushed her hand into her shoulder bag and pulled out a bar of chocolate. Simon thrust out his hand but Jenny was even faster. She withdrew it and held it just out of his reach. 'Look,' she said hastily, seeing the corners of his mouth going down again, 'this is for you but I want you to promise me something first, Simon. I want you to promise that you'll only play round here. You will, won't you?' The big head nodded heavily up and down and the hand stretched out for the chocolate again. 'Here you are then, Simon. Don't eat it all at once.'

He snatched it out of her hand and ripped the packet open so fast that the wrappings fell all over the road. He crammed the whole bar into his mouth and then dropped on all fours and carefully collected up the pieces of silver paper, chuckling as he did so, and throwing the other bits away.

'Eat it slowly, Simon,' said Jenny. 'Slowly.'

He scrabbled for the last piece of silver paper and crouched there, his mouth bulging, a look of cunning on his face, and then opened his mouth wide to show a revolting mass of mangled chocolate inside.

Jenny shook her hair and frowned. 'That's not nice, is it, Simon?' she said severely. 'You know better than that.'

He stuck out his underlip and began to crawl backwards. When he felt he was a safe distance away he got slowly and unsteadily to his feet, shook his head and shambled off.

'Simon, come back!' she shouted after him, but he lurched on up the hill without a backward glance. She shrugged. 'Oh, well, I don't suppose I'll see him again for a bit.' For the first time she looked at Mike, who was standing as if rooted to the spot, an appalled expression on his face. 'There's no need to look like that,' she said sharply. 'He's harmless enough, poor kid. Just thank your lucky stars you're not like that.'

'I—er . . . well,' Mike didn't know what to say. The sight of Simon had made him feel sick. He felt ashamed of himself but he couldn't help it. 'What's wrong with him?' he asked at last.

'He's a mongol—but I think it's complicated by something else.'

'Can't he be treated? Shouldn't he be in a hospital or something? Would it cost too much for a Gozitan family?'

'Gozitan? He's not Gozitan. He's English. His parents brought him out here to live. They didn't want him dragging out his life in an institution. They

45

thought people might be kinder out here and I reckon they're right. England's full of people like you who don't want to know, but over here they seem to think of it as—well, one of nature's calamities or an act of God or something.' She was getting more and more worked up. 'He's got every right to be free. After all, he'll die soon enough!'

'Die!' echoed Mike incredulously. 'Die! Why should he?'

'Mongols just do. They have short lives.' She paused for a moment and then gave a short, embarrassed laugh. 'Sorry I got so wound up. Come on, let's go in. You collapse and I'll get a drink.'

'Jenny,' Mike called after her as he sat down, 'what's a Band Club?'

'It's a club. Every village has one. They organize the festas, collect . . .'

'What's a festa?'

She came back, two glasses in her hands. 'What does it sound like, stupid? Every village has one. It's the celebration of their saint's day. It's a three day jamboree, partly religious and partly a fabulous jamboree.' She settled down on the floor beside him. 'Actually it's fantastic. The Band Clubs fix everything. They provide the music and the church's treasure is brought out and they parade the statue around the streets and stick it up in the square and let off fireworks . . .'

'Fireworks! I'm crazy about them.'

'Me too. They make them themselves here. They have a secret formula for them. And all the time the sky is absolutely exploding with sound. That's when they set off petards—pure gelignite, I suppose—to frighten off the devils or something like that. The Victoria festa comes off soon. That's why Freddie buzzed off, I guess.' She glanced up at Mike, who was

46

sprawled on the divan still looking exhausted. 'Look, why don't you hop into the bath?' she suggested. 'You'll feel a hell of a lot better if you do. I'll run it for you. If I chuck in a lot of salt it'll help to take off the stiffness.' She darted out of the room and called to Mike a couple of minutes later, 'Come on, it's ready.'

Mike hadn't much faith in her remedy but once he was in the water and relaxing, he had to admit that she was right. The only trouble was that the hot water made it only too easy to relax. He lay there with his eyes closed for some time and then, suddenly realizing that he was almost dropping off, he climbed out, gave himself a brisk rub down, threw on his clothes again and ran down the stairs. 'Hallo, Mario,' he exclaimed in surprise as he rounded the corner. 'I didn't hear you come.'

'You must have practically been out for the count,' Jenny remarked, 'if you couldn't hear his old Snorter puffing up the hill.'

Mario turned and looked at him gravely. He pushed a lock of straight black hair to one side. 'About York,' he began suddenly.

Just as suddenly Mike felt that he couldn't take any more football chat. His face went red. 'Look,' he said, 'I've been leading you up the garden. I don't know anything about football. I don't want to know anything about football. I couldn't care less about football. I just don't like football.' Surprised at his own outburst, he sat down heavily.

There was a long silence. 'That's torn it,' Mike said to himself. 'It's probably like sacrilege here.'

Mario got to his feet and walked slowly across the room to Mike, his brown face serious. He thrust out one hand and then clapped Mike on the back with the other. 'Great!' he cried, his face brightening. 'That's great. I really thought I'd have to spend the rest of

47

my life talking about football to every Englishman I met. I'm bored by it myself. That's really great!' He pumped away at Mike's hand and went on muttering 'Great' while they grinned at each other.

Jenny turned round. 'You said you had to go to Marselforn, Mario. Why don't you go through Xaghra and then you can give Mike a lift home?'

'Great!' they both said.

CHAPTER FOUR

'Easy, James,' said Jenny warningly, as James approached a sharp corner.

James stamped on the brakes and changed gear noisily before racing off again. 'Haven't booked,' he grunted as he overtook a lorry. 'Might not get on the ferry.'

'There's plenty of time.' Jenny turned round to Mario and Mike. 'I don't know what's got into him lately. He's always jittering around.'

'Absolute drivel!' James shot round the last bend and hurtled down to the quay. There were hardly any other cars there and within minutes they rolled on to the car deck. James led the way up to the top deck, settled down on one seat and spread the *Times of Malta* all over the one facing him.

Jenny bent over him. 'Anything in it?'

'Nothing much.' James started to turn the page over but Jenny caught his hand and pushed it back.

'Nothing much! Listen to this: "In spite of the most stringent precautions ever taken in Sicily, Benito Vesculdi, who was being taken from prison to the court where he was to have been tried on charges in the Mafia drugs case, escaped when the van he was travelling in and the police car escorting it were ambushed in the Palermo suburbs yesterday. As accusation and counter-accusations of complicity in the affair were being exchanged by the Police, the Ministry of Justice and the Ministry of the Interior, the Chief of Police offered his resignation. A full-scale inquiry has been announced by the Minister. Although the car in which Vesculdi escaped has been discovered and a house-to-house search is being conducted in Palermo, there has been no trace of him. It is believed that Vesculdi is almost certainly out of the country by now . . ." '

'Do you mind!' James flicked the page over and flattened it with a heavy hand. 'I want to see the regatta results.'

'But aren't you interested?' asked Mike in an amazed voice.

'Why should I be? He's not English, is he?' James read on while Jenny lifted her eyebrows meaningly at the others.

'I'll go and get us some coffee,' Mario said. 'They've opened up the hatch now.'

Mike settled himself next to Jenny. 'The Mafia really has got it sewn up,' he remarked.

James crackled his newspaper irritably. 'Can't you talk about anything else?' he grunted. 'You don't even know that it was anything to do with them. Nothing's been proved.'

'Oh, come on, Unc,' protested Jenny. 'Be your age.'

James snorted and slammed the paper down. He thrust back his seat and stalked away, muttering to himself.

'What's up with him?' Mario came back with the coffee in plastic cups.

Jenny shrugged. 'Dunno, really. It doesn't matter anyway. He'll get over it.'

Mike sipped his coffee and then put it down hastily, a disgusted expression on his face. He ran his tongue over his lips. 'Crikey!' he exclaimed. 'It's vile, isn't it?'

'Vile,' agreed Jenny. 'It always is.'

'Then why buy it?'

'Tradition,' she said gravely. 'A journey to Malta isn't complete without it.'

'Jenny,' Mario squatted near her. 'I ran into Caldena yesterday. He asked me if I'd seen Simon.'

'What did you say?'

'I said he was in Marselforn.'

Mike looked up sharply. 'But he wasn't,' he said. 'He was in Xlendi.'

'That's right,' agreed Mario cheerfully, and he half-raised his mug to Jenny, who smiled back at him.

Mike looked from one to the other. For just a moment he felt completely excluded, shut out from them. Then he gave himself a mental shrug. If they didn't want to let him in on something, they didn't. After all, whatever it was, it was their business, not his. There wasn't much he could do about it anyway. 'What are we going to do in Malta?' he asked after a bit.

'We can go with James to start with,' suggested Jenny. 'I quite like going round the Marina with him.'

'What's that?' James's perambulation had brought him back to them again. 'Oh, no,' he said firmly, 'you're not coming with me.'

'But why not?' she cried. 'You don't usually mind.'

James peered down at her long legs. 'Your skirt's too short. They won't listen to me while you're flaunting yourself about.'

'Flaunting!' Jenny went pink with indignation. 'I don't do anything of the sort. You know I don't.'

'Well, you're not hanging round my neck today. I've got too much to do.' He ran his hand through his shaggy hair in a distracted way. 'I don't mind meeting you later though.'

'Thanks, that's really big of you, James,' Jenny said sarcastically.

He plonked his big hand down on her shoulder. 'That's all right,' he said in a pleased voice. 'I'll tell you what, let's meet at the Phoenicia for lunch at about

one. I'll know by then which ferry I want to catch
back. Come on,' he added as the ship grated her way
alongside, 'Let's get below. I don't want to hang
around.'

Once they were off the boat James drove in a more
relaxed manner towards Valletta. Mike caught himself
gazing around almost open-mouthed at the teeming
streets. He hadn't realized before just how remote Gozo
was, for all its nearness to Malta. In comparison with it
Malta was positively humming with life.

Jenny nudged him. 'Shall we do the sights first?'

'The sights?' It took Mike a moment or two to catch
on. 'Sure. Fine. Is there much to see?'

'Is there much to see?' Mario looked at him in
disbelief. 'What a question! Don't you know anything
about Malta?'

'Well,' said Mike hesitantly, 'I know there was a
siege. That was when the knights slogged it out for a
bit, wasn't it?'

'Slogged it out for a bit!' Jenny's voice was passion-
ate. 'That bit lasted for a hundred and eighteen days. A
hundred and eighteen searingly hot summer days—
days when it was roasting, when the air was sizzling
and they found it difficult even to breathe. There were
something like seven hundred knights and they held the
fortresses against forty thousand Turks. They did
have several thousand Maltese on their side but they
had nothing in the way of weapons—only what they
could make or take from the dead. But the Turks were
really well organized. They had everything—cannon,
food, ammunition, supplies, reserves, the lot—while the
knights and the Maltese were sealed up, without any
real hope of reinforcements. The Turks did offer the
Maltese an amnesty but they wouldn't leave. They
chose to stay inside those crumbling walls and fight—
everybody fought: men, women and children, in one of

the bloodiest sieges ever known. The knights had to
fight. They had to fight to the last man. There wasn't
anywhere for them to go. They either had to defeat the
Turks or die—and most of them died. By the time the
siege was raised practically everyone had been badly
wounded, more than once, most of them. They were a
tiny company of cripples.'

Mike leaned back. In his imagination he saw it
all—knights, Maltese, and Turks—in flowing robes, in
armour, in padded leather, with swords and scimitars
and daggers, fighting it out hand to hand, day after
day, under a hot, blistering sun, with the din of cannon
and the roar of explosives constantly in their ears. The
hordes of the Ottoman Empire sweeping up in endless
waves to the walls, the desperate defenders hurling
them back time and time again—and always the utter
conviction of defenders and attackers alike of the
rightness of their cause and the absolute certainty that
they would find salvation in their death.

Jenny watched Mike's face. 'It's fantastic, isn't it?'
she said. Mike nodded.

Mario leaned forward. 'Let's show him Valletta
first,' he suggested.

James slammed the brakes on so hard that they were
flung on top of each other. 'Stop gabbling,' he rumbled.
'This is where you get off.'

'But this is Sliema,' protested Jenny. 'We want to go
to Valletta.'

'Too bad.' He grabbed hold of Jenny's arm as they
reluctantly climbed out. 'Listen, there's something I
want you to do for me. Old Commander Jonson's
things are being auctioned today at his house. I want
you to go and bid for a couple of things for me. I'd like
his old telescope and his globe.' He thrust a couple of
crumpled five-pound notes into her hand. 'I don't know
what they'll go for. Just do your best.' He threw the

Land-Rover into gear and edged out into the traffic, leaving a furious Jenny standing in the road.

'What's up?' Mario gripped her elbow and steered her on to the pavement.

'It's James—he's a dirty rat!'

'What's he done now?'

'Loused up our day,' she said bitterly. 'Now we've got to spend the whole morning at some dreary old auction.' Furiously she stomped off and the boys followed her. She turned off the main road and marched up a small alley, weaving her way in and out of the crowds at such a rate that Mike, who stopped every now and again to peer into the bazaar-like shops, was forced to break into a little trot in order to keep up with her.

At last they came into a small square and she made for a narrow house in the corner and ran up the steps. Suddenly she clapped both hands to her head in a gesture of astonishment, and swung round. 'Well,' she said, almost speechless. 'Well.'

'What do you mean?' Mario bounded up the steps to her side.

She pointed at the closed door. 'There isn't any auction. The place is locked up.'

Mario squinted through the letter-box. 'That's right, it is. It's empty. Wait a minute though.' He darted down the steps again and rushed up to a postman who was strolling past and had a rapid conversation in Maltese with him. Then he hurtled back to Mike and Jenny. 'There *is* an auction,' he said, 'but it's not being held here. It's at the Pharaoh.'

'The Pharaoh?' Mike turned his enquiring face to him.

'It's a hotel—a big one,' Mario explained. 'It's a funny thing to do though, isn't it?'

'Is it? I don't know. No, I don't suppose it is. If there

are a lot of people interested in it then this house wouldn't really be big enough.' Jenny looked at the boys. 'Well, what shall we do? Personally, I've just about had it—or rather James has. I couldn't care less about his globe.'

Mike looked from one to the other. 'I think we ought to try to get it for him,' he said awkwardly. 'It's a bit mean not to.'

'He's right,' said Mario firmly. 'Let's go there.'

Jenny pursed her lips. 'Okay,' she said at last, 'but let's take a taxi on James. I'm not slogging around on foot for him—not in this heat.'

By the time they got to the Pharaoh and into the room off the lobby where the auction was being held, there was hardly room for them to get in. Jenny wriggled her way through the crowds to the front and came back a few minutes later looking flushed and cross. She brushed aside the wispy bits of hair that clung to her face. 'Hell! I might have guessed. It's being conducted in Maltese.'

Several people, indignant looks on their faces, turned round and hissed at her to be quiet. Mario edged closer. 'Tell me what you want. I'll do the bidding for you.' Jenny whispered quickly in his ear and thrust the money into his hands.

Once he had gone she stared glumly at her feet and shuffled them loudly across the polished floor, humming to herself at the same time. As yet more people turned round, Mike took her arm and led her out into the entrance lobby. 'There's no point in hanging about there,' he said. 'Mario's no fool. He'll cope.'

'Let's wait in the lounge then,' Jenny suggested, pushing the door open. 'It's a bit more comfortable in there.' Once she was settled in a chair she began to cheer up. 'When this is over,' she began, 'we'll start on the conducted tour. There still ought to be enough time.' She glanced through the open door to the reception desk. 'Police,' she remarked casually. 'Two of them. Somebody's scarpered without paying, I guess.'

Mike had wandered right across the room to the windows and was looking out across the verandah to the Grand Harbour. 'What a fantastic view!'

Jenny jumped up from her chair. 'You ought to see it from the roof garden. I wonder if we've got time to go up there now?'

'You have—all the time in the world.' Mario, a disgruntled expression on his face, strolled in. They both looked up hopefully at him, but he shook his head. 'No go,' he said, pushing back the lock of hair that fell in his eyes. 'The globe had already gone and the telescope fetched over twenty.'

'Blast!' Jenny slammed her head against the doorpost. 'We've wasted the whole damn morning for nothing.' She suddenly snatched the money from Mario's fingers. 'I'm not leaving empty-handed, I can tell you that!' She rushed out of the lounge, leaving Mario looking after her, an amused smile on his lips.

'What's come over her?' asked Mike.

'She's lost her cool. It makes her seem a bit more normal somehow, doesn't it?'

They hung around for a few more minutes and Mike said at last, 'Shouldn't we go and drag her away? The mood she's in probably means she'll come away with a house full of furniture.'

'She might at that.'

The crowd had thinned considerably by the time they got back and they could clearly see Jenny thrusting up her hand over and over again. 'She's bidding for that crate of old china,' Mike whispered. 'She must be out of her mind.'

'It doesn't look up to much.' Mario got near enough to take hold of Jenny's hand and force it down. 'What

do you think you're doing?' he muttered. 'The price is
over twenty-five pounds already.'

She tugged her hand free. 'Mind your own
business,' she snapped, her eyes on the auctioneer.

'Come on, Jenny,' said Mike, 'be reasonable.' Her
blue eyes flashed furiously at him and in that instant
of inattention the china was knocked down to a
delighted woman.

Jenny flung herself round and stamped. 'That was
Crown Derby!' she cried. 'It was early stuff, I know it
was. It was worth a packet. James would have paid. I
knew what I was doing. You're just a couple of
blundering fools!' Tears suddenly appeared in her eyes
and brushing them aside she rushed out of the room.

Mike and Mario stood side by side looking guiltily
at each other. 'Do you know,' said Mike, 'I've got a
feeling that she was right.'

'Hell's bells!' groaned Mario. 'Can't we make it up
to her somehow?' The auctioneer's assistant staggered
past, an old zinc bath in his arms, and put it down
heavily near the rostrum. The auctioneer, a bored look
on his face, peered into it and selected a couple of
tattered books and a teapot and held them up. No one
seemed interested. 'Two shillings,' said Mario to Mike.
'They must be worth more than that.'

The bidding dragged on for another couple of
minutes and then Mike, with a sudden air of resolution, raised his hand and the auctioneer thankfully
banged down his gavel.

Mike was staggered. He hadn't really meant to do it
at all. He couldn't think what had come over him.
'How much has it cost me?' he asked anxiously.

'A pound—I'll split it with you though,' said Mario
generously. 'Maybe the books will be worth it.'

'Cripes! A pound!' Mike put his hand into his
pocket and then, as the assistant approached, a look of

horror crossed his face. 'Crikey! I thought I was bidding for the teapot and the books. We've got the lot!'

Mario handed his share of the money over and lifted the heavy bath. 'We're just a couple of mugs,' he said as they staggered out into the lobby to where Jenny was sitting, staring morosely across the room. 'Jenny,' he went on in a depressed voice. 'We've bought you a present.'

Jenny, her face still miserable, looked over her shoulder and saw Mario half-hidden under the bath while a shamefaced Mike stood at his shoulder clutching a saucepan with a hole in it. She stared at them in disbelief for a moment and then she threw back her head and suddenly laughed, her eyes sparkling. Mike stared at her and then glanced at Mario's dismal face and spluttered too, and after a second Mario joined in too. The three of them giggled and reeled around while the few other occupants of the lobby looked on with stiff disapproval.

Eventually they grew quieter. 'Put it down here,' Jenny gasped at last. She looked at it again. 'No, maybe I'm wrong. Perhaps the dustbin's the best place for it.'

'The dustbin!' Mike was outraged. 'We've just paid a quid for it.'

'Then you were robbed.' She caught a glimpse of their disappointed faces and relented. 'Okay, drop it, Mario. I'll have a quick look through. We'll leave anything we don't want behind.' She looked up at the reception clerk's anxious face. 'Don't worry,' she said. 'We'll be two minutes.' Ruthlessly she sorted through the bath and put a small miscellaneous collection of things on one side. 'We'll decide about these later,' she said decisively. 'Mario, do you think you could take these back to the auction room and persuade them to lose them for us? I'm going to take Mike up to the roof garden. See you up there.'

Mario picked up the bath again. 'No, I'll wait here. I'll see you when you come down.'

Jenny quickly scooped up everything she'd picked up and put them into the arms of the astonished hall porter. 'You'll look after them, won't you?' she said persuasively, smiling up into his eyes. 'We won't be a moment, honestly. We're just going up to the roof garden.'

'The roof garden?' The reception clerk looked up quickly. 'I'm sorry. It is closed. We are only doing lunch in the restaurant today.'

'But we're not going there for lunch. I want to show him the view.'

A tall quiet man unrolled himself from a deep chair and stood up. 'I'm afraid the lifts are out of action for a few hours,' he said.

'What, all of them?' Jenny looked at him with disbelief.

'All of them,' he repeated. 'Something to do with the generator.'

Jenny stared at him. 'Are you the manager then?' she demanded.

He bowed his head slightly. 'Yes, I'm in charge.'

Jenny turned to Mike. 'Fancy slogging up five floors?' she asked.

The receptionist leaned across the desk. 'We are asking people who are not residents not to use the main staircase,' he said awkwardly. 'You see there would be . . .'

'Congestion,' finished the other man. 'Sounds stupid, I know, but you know what fire regulations are like. Too bad, I'm afraid.'

'Yes,' said Jenny thoughtfully. 'It's too bad.' She went off into the lounge followed by Mike and once they were out of sight of the desk she hustled him across to a small plain door in the far wall. It led to a narrow carpeted staircase. Mike hung back. 'Where are we going?'

'To the roof garden,' she said, a note of surprise in her voice. 'I said I'd show it to you. Come on. These are the service stairs. We aren't likely to run into anyone at this time.' They ran up several flights before Jenny stopped for breath. 'Only two more,' she puffed.

Mike stood there taking deep breaths. 'Three, I think.'

'No, two,' she said firmly as they plodded on and then, as they neared the top of the stairs she paused. 'Right. I only hope you think it's worth it.'

'So do I,' he panted.

Jenny stopped at last, her face hot and shiny. 'Success,' she said, a confident smile on her face, as she pushed open the door and put her head out. Mike saw her face change. The colour drained away as she stood there transfixed, her mouth slightly open and her eyes wide. Mike grasped the door from her fingers and poked his head out. It was like something out of a film. Two policemen, guns in their hands and covered by two others, hurled themselves at that very moment at a locked door and as they did so two shots crackled, two neat holes were drilled in the door and one of the policemen fell awkwardly against the wall and slumped very slowly to the ground, a dark mark spreading rapidly across his shirt.

As the second man burst through the door Jenny turned and fled noiselessly down the stairs. Mike was rooted to the spot. He couldn't have moved if he'd wanted to. Suddenly the corridor was alive with people. A policeman grabbed him. 'Get out!' he snapped. 'Keep your mouth shut. It's not over yet,' and he pushed Mike back out of sight.

Jenny stumbled down the stairs, across the lounge and into the lobby and fell into James's arms. 'James!' she cried. 'It's horrible up there. Someone's been shot—a policeman. I saw the blood dribble out of him. It's horrible.'

James's face went white. He put his arm round Jenny's shoulder. 'It's all right, Jenny,' he said. 'It's all right.' He led her over to a chair. 'Now tell me about it. What happened?'

Jenny pushed the hair from her face and gave him a feeble smile. 'It's just that it was so unexpected,' she said. 'There was Mike and me expecting to walk out on to the roof garden and when we pushed open the door there we were in the middle of a B-type flicker.'

Mario hovered round her as she went on with the story. 'Who were they shooting at?'

'I don't know. Whoever it was he fired first.' She suddenly stared about her. 'Where's Mike?'

'Coming.' Mario pointed to the lounge as Mike, his face serious, walked across to them. 'Who was it?'

Mike shook his head. 'I don't know. The police hustled me off. They said to keep quiet about it.'

Jenny put her hand to her mouth. 'I've been . . .' She looked at James and Mario. 'Oh, well, I don't suppose you two count though.'

Mike turned to James. 'It's lucky you're here,' he remarked.

'Lucky?' repeated James. 'What's lucky about that? I told you we were having lunch here.'

'Oh, James, you didn't,' protested Jenny. 'You said the Phoenicia not the Pharaoh, didn't he?' She turned appealingly to the boys and they both nodded.

'Oh my God!' exclaimed James. 'It just goes to show. You just don't listen to a word I say. I might just as well save my breath.'

As they moved towards the restaurant the doorman

hurried after Jenny and thrust a carrier bag into her hands. 'Oh, thanks a lot,' she said. 'I'd forgotten about them.'

James peered at the bag suspiciously. 'What's in there then?'

'Mike and Mario bought me some things at the auction.'

'What about me then?' he asked.

'No luck. You hadn't given us anything like enough money.'

'Thought I hadn't,' he grunted as he sat down and reached for the menu.

'Oh, James!' they said.

As James dug into his avocado he pulled an old envelope from his pocket and jotted some figures down on it, shook his head and started all over again. Suddenly, half-way through the meal, he jumped up. 'Must make a phone call,' he said. 'Won't be a minute. You carry on.'

James's minute stretched into half an hour and still he didn't come back. Jenny pushed the coffee cups away and dragged out the carrier bag from under her chair. 'Let's have a look,' she said, putting everything on the table. 'I'll tell you what, let's each have two of these little spoons and . . .'

'But they're yours,' Mike protested. 'We bought them for you.'

She took no notice and waved a rusty old egg-whisk in the air. 'Any takers? No? Then it's mine. You can have this little penknife, Mike, and . . .'

'I don't really want it. I've got one already.'

'So have I,' Mario said, picking it up and examining it, 'but it's not as nice as this.'

'Right then, that's settled. You'd better take something, Mike.'

Mike looked dubiously at the books. 'I don't think they'll be any good to me. They're cookery books.'

'Cookery books!' Jenny was pleased. 'Now they're something I'd really like,' she said, and the boys exchanged gratified looks with each other.

Mike picked up an old Edward VII coronation mug. 'I wouldn't mind having this.'

'Fine. Then that only leaves this old kaleidoscope. Who fancies it? No one? Oh, well, I'll take it for Simon. He'll probably love it.' Jenny arranged everything in a neat row and smiled. 'It wasn't such a bad morning's work after all.' As she thumbed through a hefty cookery book a thick folded piece of paper fell out.

Mario unfolded it carefully and spread it out. 'Look!' he said. 'It's an old map of Gozo.'

'Is it Gozo?' asked Jenny. 'It doesn't look quite right somehow.'

'That's probably because it *is* old,' remarked Mike, leaning across the table to get a better look. 'You can tell by the writing. No one does loops and squiggles like that now.'

'I wonder just how old it is,' said Jenny. 'I'd like to know.'

'What's that?' James came back into the restaurant and sat down. 'Oh, a map. You ought to show it to Caldena. He's in the lounge. I just ran into him. Isn't he supposed to be hot stuff on maps?'

'Of course he is,' began Mike eagerly, but his voice died away as he caught a glimpse of Jenny and Mario's stony faces.

James signalled for coffee. 'Fortunate I bumped into him. He was here for the auction too and . . .'

Jenny looked up sharply. 'No, he wasn't,' she said.

'He might have been,' said Mike. 'You probably just didn't notice him.'

'I'm positive he wasn't there. I always know when he's around. I can feel it,' she insisted.

'Balderdash!' snorted James.

Mario saw Jenny's face go red. 'How did you get on at the Marina, James?' he asked quickly. 'Is the boat ready?'

'Of course it isn't,' he said impatiently. 'I'd have probably dropped dead with shock if it had been.' He pulled the envelope out again and stared hard at the figures he'd written down.

'Then why did you bother to come to Malta today?'

'What?' James looked up blankly. 'Oh, if I didn't put in an appearance they'd never get on with it. Still, it's a damned nuisance.'

Jenny looked at him suspiciously. For a man who'd just been let down he was remarkably cheerful. She leaned across him and peered at the envelope and frowned. James quickly screwed it up and shoved it into a pocket. 'James,' she said, 'what have you been up to?'

'Me?' James assumed an air of innocence that fooled no one. He drummed his fingers on the table and stared vacantly up at the ceiling.

'Come on, James, come clean. You'll have to tell me sooner or later.' Jenny assumed the patient air of a mother dealing with a naughty child.

James wriggled around a bit. 'Don't know what . . .' He shot her a look out of the corner of his eyes and gave a sudden mischievous grin. 'You'll find out soon enough.'

Jenny looked puzzled for a moment or two and then she gasped and leaned forward and stared directly into his eyes. 'You've bought another boat!' she said accusingly.

James big round face went bright red. He fingered his chin nervously. 'Not exactly *bought* . . .'

'James!' Her voice became shriller and the few people remaining in the restaurant looked up in surprise.

'Take it easy,' he said. 'What's all the fuss about? Even if I had, and I'm not saying I have, mark you, what's wrong with that? It's my . . .'

'James!' she cried despairingly. 'You've already got a yacht . . .'

'Can't use it,' he muttered sulkily.

'You're not exactly a millionaire, James. You haven't got the sort of money to run two boats. What the hell do you want another for anyway?'

'It's not a yacht.' James looked like a little boy who's hit a conker dead on target.

'Then what . . .?'

He waggled a large finger at her. 'Guess!' he said playfully.

'James!' she shouted furiously.

'Haven't actually bought it,' he mumbled. 'Just having it for a trial run.'

'Having what?'

'Only a motor launch,' he gabbled swiftly. 'You see, what with the Med being so tricky and . . .'

'A motor launch!' Jenny's eyes sparkled dangerously.

'Only a little one, Jen,' he said pacifically.

'Don't call me Jen!' she shouted.

'More like a rowing boat really, with just a little engine . . .'

'James, if you . . .'

There was a sudden silence in the restaurant and Mike looked furtively around. Everyone was staring at them. He hunched himself up. In his family people just didn't have rows. A bit of polite disagreeing was about all that went on—and never in public. He glanced at Mario and found that he was clearly enjoying every moment of it.

Suddenly, as Jenny launched into yet another attack, Mike felt he couldn't take any more and so he slipped off his chair and made his way out to the lobby at the same moment as Caldena came out of the lounge.

'Nice to see you, Mike,' Caldena said as he came over. 'I hear that you were mixed up in that nasty business upstairs.'

Mike frowned. 'How did you know?'

Caldena looked serious. 'James told me, of course. I must say that it's a relief they've caught Vesculdi.'

'Vesculdi? Was that who it was?' said Mike excitedly. 'I wonder how they got on to him? I mean, he wouldn't just have signed the register with his own name, would he?'

Caldena gave a quick little smile. 'I don't suppose he would.' He looked over Mike's shoulder. 'Hallo again, James,' he said.

James beamed at him but Mario and Jenny stared back in a hostile way. Jenny turned round as if to go out and the map slipped to the ground. Caldena bent and picked it up. 'That's interesting,' he remarked. 'Where did you get that, Jenny?'

She came back and deliberately tweaked it from his fingers. 'Do you mind?' she said coldly. 'It's private,' and she swept out of the hotel leaving an astounded Caldena behind her.

Mike caught her up. 'Do you always have to be so bitchy to Caldena?' he hissed.

'Bitchy?' repeated Jenny. 'Yes, that's a good way of putting it,' and she relapsed into silence for the rest of the drive to the ferry.

CHAPTER FIVE

The following morning Mike trudged up the steeply sloping hill that led from Victoria to the Citadel. By the time he reached the top he was beginning to sweat and he was breathing heavily. Eventually he entered the square and looked up at the vast cathedral and the flight of wide steps leading up to it. He shook his head. He really hadn't the strength to climb those as well. He'd look at the cathedral another time. The law courts, impressive, solid-looking buildings, were on one side and a beautifully restored house, the museum, on the other. There were a few more houses, it seemed, in the narrow street at the side of the cathedral, and that seemed to be that.

He turned and walked alongside one of the walls. There was a fantastic panoramic view of the island from it and he rested his arms on the chest-high wall and looked down at the sheer drop below. How on earth, he wondered, had anyone worked up the nerve to swing down on a rope? It was a strange feeling being up there. It was a bit like being marooned on an island for all that Victoria, busy, noisy and bustling with people, was immediately below. He drifted along a few more yards and then stopped to admire an old cannon that poked its threatening nose through an embrasure and rubbed his hand along the smooth barrel.

'Who are you gunning for?'

Mike swivelled round and saw Mario's amused

face. 'Just admiring,' he replied. 'It's an incredible thing, isn't it? Look at the engraving on it.'

Mario gave it a friendly pat. 'Guns really meant something then. The craftsmanship was fantastic.' He glanced at his watch. 'Let's go back to the square and see if Jenny's made it yet.'

'What are we supposed to be doing here?' asked Mike.

'I think it's the map,' said Mario and they strolled along together. 'She simply can't bear not to know about things. She worries away at all sorts of piffling things until she really understands and then she loses interest. She probably wants to show it to the curator to see what he makes of it.'

'Look, there she is.' Mike raised his hand and waved at the small figure toiling up the hill.

'Hi!' said Jenny breathlessly as she appeared round the last bend. 'Sorry I'm late. Let's go straight in to the curator.' As she fished in her old shoulder bag for a thick brown envelope, Mario winked at Mike.

She marched into the cool shady house followed by the boys. Mike would have liked to stop and have a look round but Mario pushed him along until they reached an inner room where a quiet, intelligent-looking man was peacefully turning a fragment of pottery over and over in his hand. He smiled and got up as they entered and there were great hand-shakings all round. 'Of course,' Mr Alberghini said to Mike, 'I know your father well. He is a really great scholar.' And he beamed away again. 'Now what can I do for you?'

Jenny produced her envelope and handed the map over and rattled through the story of how she got it. 'Hm!' Mr Alberghini took it over to his desk and switched on a powerful light and then put his glasses on. 'Yes,' he said at last, 'it's quite interesting. You are right about one thing. It is a map of Gozo. There can't be much doubt about that. It's nineteenth century, I should think.'

'Oh!' Jenny's face fell. 'Not earlier?'

'I really don't think so.' He held the paper high under the light and peered closely at it. 'It's most unlikely to be earlier. No, unless I'm very much mistaken it's part of a nineteenth-century chart.'

'What do you mean—a part of a chart?'

He pointed to one side. 'Look at this edge. I should think that the rest of it was simply sliced off at some stage.'

'But what do you think the other part was of?' asked Mario peering over his shoulder.

Mr Alberghini raised his head and smiled. 'You don't have to be much of a detective to answer that one. I should guess that it was a map of Malta. The writing on it is Italian . . .'

'Italian!' Mike exclaimed.

'Of course. It's not really surprising. Indeed, many of our early records are kept in Naples or Palermo.'

Mike pointed at a couple of faded names. 'But that's Arabic, isn't it?'

'Yes. After all, when you think about it you'll realize that the Arabs have been raiding and trading in the Mediterranean for centuries so a lot of the names are bound to be Arabic. The hand, however, is certainly Italian. That's really as much as I can possibly tell you, I'm afraid. There is one person who might—just might—be able to tell you a little more, and that is Signor Caldena. He really has become an expert, so if you'll let me . . .'

'No!' said Jenny sharply. She picked it up again and put it carefully back into the envelope. She stopped for a moment, realizing how rude she must have seemed. 'Sorry,' she said, 'I would have left it with you but it's just that James is waiting for me. You see, he's quite interested in maps himself and so I promised to let him have it next to compare it with one he's got.'

'James! But he couldn't care... Ouch!' Mike glared at Jenny and rubbed his ankle. 'What ...'

'James was only saying last night that he'd get his out first thing this morning,' Jenny continued smoothly.

'Of course.' Mr Alberghini took his glasses off and gave them a thorough polish. 'Let me know if you find out any more about it, won't you?'

'Sure, and thanks for being so patient.' Jenny gave him a warm smile as she led the way out, while Mike hobbled along in the rear.

'What's the idea?' he exploded as soon as they were outside. 'You trying to cripple me or something?'

'Don't be silly. I just wasn't going to have Caldena getting his dirty paws on it.'

'And what's so special about it? Do you think it's going to lead you to a treasure trove or something?'

'What do you take me for? An idiot?' Jenny went pink. Actually, deep down she had had a very slight hope that it might have proved to be really old and valuable in some way. What it was she had hoped for she wasn't quite sure, but she wasn't going to admit anything to Mike and Mario. 'I just wanted to know a bit more about it, that was all.'

'Then why get so upset just because Caldena was mentioned?' Mike asked. He looked at each of them in turn. They had on the same blank looks that came over their faces whenever he mentioned Caldena. He mooched over to the wall and leaned moodily against it. Mario and Jenny looked at each other and Jenny moved across to him.

'Sorry, Mike,' she said, 'but honestly, until we've . . .'

'All right. Don't go on about it. I don't want to know.' Mike moved slightly away from her.

'I say.' Mario bent almost double over the wall. 'That's Simon down there.' As Jenny automatically moved closer to look Mario straightened up and held up one arm as a barrier. 'Take it easy,' he said.

She smiled at him and turned to Mike, who had himself moved across to them. 'I'm no good at heights,' she said. 'I can't look down. Silly, isn't it?'

'I don't know,' said Mike, having got over his momentary ill-humour as they went down the hill, 'everybody's got something. Lots of people are scared stiff in planes and others become gibbering idiots at the idea of being shut in.'

'My aunt's still afraid of the dark,' said Mario, 'and she's sixty-seven. She won't go to bed unless she's got a night-light by her bed.' He steered them all into a long narrow café. 'Let's have a drink.'

A small man, his wrinkled face creased up into a perpetual smile, his long white apron almost reaching to the ground, met them at the door. He dusted down a table with a teacloth. 'Nice to see you,' he said. 'It's a good day, huh? I shall get you some tea.'

Mike turned to Jenny. 'Do you want tea?' he asked.

She grinned back at him. 'That's got absolutely nothing to do with it,' she said. 'If Arthur's decided we're having tea, we're having tea.'

Arthur not only made it, he sat down companionably with them while they had it. He looked enquiringly at Mike and Mario hastily introduced them. 'Mike,' he said, 'is Mr Bennet's son.'

'Ah! Mr Bennet! You look like him.' He seized Mike's hand and shook it violently up and down and then he suddenly stopped. He turned to Mario. 'Who is Mr Bennet?' he asked.

'You know, Mr Bennet the writer in Xaghra.'

'Ah!' Arthur pumped away again. 'Very nice man,' he said as he dropped it at last. 'Very nice man,' he repeated enthusiastically and Mike hastily put his hand under the table out of reach. Arthur leaned back and lit a cigarette. 'And how was Malta yesterday?' he said to Jenny. 'You had a good trip?'

'Were you on the ferry?' asked Mike. Arthur shook his head and blew a smoke ring. 'Then how . . .?'

'Everyone knows everything on Gozo,' said Mario. 'There's no such thing as a secret life.'

'Isn't there? Some people seem to manage it all right,' said Jenny meaningly, and much to his annoyance Mike saw one of their conspiratorial glances pass between them. Fortunately, just at that moment, two Englishmen came in before he had a chance to snap back.

Arthur jumped to his feet. 'You do not know each other?' he asked as they all stared. 'Then you must meet.' He stood between the two sides like a referee. He tapped each of them on the head in turn. 'Jenny and Mario and Mike,' he said. Then he turned to the newcomers. 'This is Al,' he said, indicating the taller man with dark hair, 'and Nick,' and he pointed at the freckle-faced one. 'They are new to Gozo but they like it. Excuse me. I will get you tea.'

The freckle-faced man grinned. 'You've got us round the wrong way, Arthur,' he said. 'I'm Al. This is Nick.'

Nick ran his hand over his smooth head. 'Arthur's right when he calls us new though. We only got here yesterday.'

'What was it like in England?' asked Mike.

'All right, a bit chilly. Not like this,' and they all looked out at the sun-baked street.

'Have you come for a holiday?' asked Mario.

'Well, yes and no,' replied Al. 'Actually we rather thought we'd like to buy a little place between us for holidays, you know.'

'So here we are,' Nick went on, 'flashing our wads of money around and celebrating our release.'

'Release?' Mario frowned. 'Release from what?'

Al laughed. 'Not what you're thinking,' he said. 'Our release from the services. We've both been stomping around what's left of the empire for the last twelve years, showing the flag and all that, and now we're free—free to indulge our whims and fancies . . .'

'Within reason,' added Nick hastily.

'Within reason,' agreed Al, 'so we shall be whizzing around in our hired limousine looking for a likely house.'

'There's quite a lot on the market,' remarked Jenny, as she slung her bag on her shoulder, 'but most of them need a lot doing to them.' The boys followed her to the door where she turned round again. 'See you around, I guess. Where are you staying?'

'At St Patrick's,' said Nick.

'Then we won't be able to help bashing into each other. I live down there too.'

They stood on the pavement outside Arthur's for a moment or two. Jenny shaded her eyes with her hand and suddenly pointed. 'There's Simon again—on the other side of the square. He shouldn't be there. We'd better catch him and take him home.'

They were just about to cross the road when Simon, who was lurching along, his head wobbling uncontrollably from side to side, looked up and caught sight of someone. 'Cal . . . Cal . . .' he shouted excitedly. 'Ciggy . . . Cal!' As his face stretched into a smile and he started to run, he somehow slipped, cannoned into a lamp-post and fell into the street.

A lorry screeched to a halt as he went sprawling into the gutter and a white-faced, frightened driver looked out of the cab. Jenny, heedless of the traffic, rushed straight across the square and knelt by Simon, who was lying there, trembling violently, with great sobs shaking the whole of his body. His face was covered with his hands and a little trickle of blood ran down his left leg.

The driver scrambled down from his lorry. 'It wasn't my fault,' he said over and over again. 'It wasn't my fault.' He turned to the crowd that was gathering around. 'There was nothing I could do. He fell under the wheels. You saw. You all saw. I couldn't help it.'

Jenny tried to take Simon's hands away from his face. 'Simon,' she said, 'it's Jenny. It's all right, Simon. Let me have a look.'

Simon continued to shudder and sob while the driver turned and appealed to the crowd once again. 'I couldn't help it. It wasn't my fault,' he repeated as they closed in on Simon.

Another car pulled up just behind the lorry and as Jenny looked up distractedly the worried look on her face suddenly changed to one of relief. 'Sue!' she exclaimed thankfully.

Sue stood and surveyed the scene for just a moment. 'It's all right, Jenny,' she said as she knelt down. 'Simon! Stop that noise. That will do.' Almost immediately he quietened down a little, but his body went on trembling. 'Show me your hands,' she said firmly. 'No, both of them. That's right. Now stretch . . .'

Now that someone more capable than herself had taken over, Jenny knelt back on her heels and saw for the first time the huge crowd that had gathered. There they all were, talking, shouting, explaining, arguing, all gathered in a tight circle round Simon. 'Please,' she said, 'please go away.' But if anything, they seemed to get even closer. Sue took no notice but went on talking quietly and reassuringly to Simon, managing to examine him fairly closely at the same time.

'More frightened than hurt,' she said at last to Jenny. 'He's got a nasty graze. That's where the blood is coming from. But that's about all. Mario, help me to get him to my car.' Together they succeeded in getting him on his feet, but as he saw the curious faces of the crowd surrounding him he hid his face in his hands. 'Aah, Aaah!' he cried.

For the first time Sue lost her air of serenity. 'Get out of the way!' she said fiercely, and the crowd suddenly fell silent and parted for her. She settled the still quivering Simon in the car and went over to the lorry driver who still looked badly shaken. 'It's all right,' she said. 'He's not hurt. I doubt if you touched him. You'd better report it to the police though.' As she smiled reassuringly at him, his strained face lost some of its tension. 'Jenny here saw everything. She's going there too. She knows you weren't to blame.'

His anxious look slowly disappeared and he nodded understandingly at her. Sue turned back to Jenny. 'I'll take him back home and explain what happened to his mother. You'd better go straight to the police station while everything's clear in your mind.'

Just as she was getting into the car beside Simon, Mike rushed up. 'Here you are, Simon,' he said. 'Look what I've got for you.'

Simon took his hands away from his tear-streaked face. His eyes lit up as they spotted the bar of chocolate Mike was holding in his hands and he grabbed it. 'Choc!' he mumbled as he ripped it open.

'Slowly, Simon. Eat it slowly,' said Jenny automatically, as Sue let in the clutch and drove very carefully away.

The policeman dealt very efficiently with them all. 'I shouldn't think you'll hear any more about it,' he said to the lorry driver. 'There seems to be no doubt about what actually happened.' He rested his chin on the back of his hands as he leant across his desk and looked at Jenny. 'I don't suppose you know what made him dash along like that?' he asked.

Jenny hesitated for a moment. 'No,' she said slowly, 'no, I'm not sure,' and Mike shot her a sharp look but said nothing.

It wasn't until they were all strolling down the Xlendi road that Mario suddenly remarked, 'Was it Caldena, Jenny?'

Jenny nodded. 'I think so. I'm pretty sure that that was what Simon was shouting about, and what's more I'm positive that I saw Caldena's Fiat parked in the square.'

'He said "Cal" and then he shouted "Ciggy", I heard him,' said Mike positively. 'Why didn't you tell the police?'

Jenny came to a halt. 'Tell them what?' she demanded. 'That Simon was chasing after Caldena? What if he was? It's hardly a criminal offence, now is it?'

They walked on for a bit in silence. 'What do you think he meant by "Ciggy"?' asked Mike eventually.

Jenny glanced quickly at Mario and he nodded back at her. 'I know you think I've just got a thing about Caldena,' she began, 'but there's a bit more to it than just ordinary dislike. I think Caldena's been feeding Simon cigarettes for some time.'

'Cigarettes? Giving cigarettes to Simon?' Mike

looked from one to the other. 'You have to be joking!'

'No, we've both seen him with them and Freddie actually saw Caldena hand a packet of something to Simon. He told me and I chased after him, but he'd got a good start. Anyway, I don't suppose I'd have caught him. He's not very good on the flat but he scrambles up the cliffs like a goat.'

'Caldena must be mad!' Mike exclaimed. 'That kid's got it tough enough as it is without being encouraged to smoke. What a lousy thing to do! He must have a twisted mind or something.'

'The trouble is,' said Mario slowly, 'we are not sure what sort of cigarettes they are.'

'What does it matter...' began Mike, and then he stopped as a horrified look spread over his face. 'What do you—? You can't mean...'

Mario's eyes narrowed. 'That's the trouble, we can't be certain. Jenny's managed to get hold of one of the packets. It's got "Prepared for S. Caldena" lightly pencilled in Italian on it.'

Mike wrinkled his brow. 'Listen, would he be fool enough to let his name be written on a packet of cigarettes if they contained hash?' he argued. 'It's not very likely, now is it?'

'We've already thought of that and the one thing Caldena isn't is a fool, that's for sure. Jenny's packet was as clean as a whistle. There wasn't a trace of anything in it, not a shred, not even a whiff, nothing. It might have contained anything from hash to hairgrips.'

'What I did think though,' said Jenny, 'was that if he'd had a batch of those packets, his name might only have been on the top one and so it's just possible he overlooked it, especially since it's written so lightly on it.'

77

'But look here,' said Mike, 'surely you ought to go to the police. After all, even though there's only the slightest suspicion, you can't possibly do any harm.'

'And I shouldn't think we'd do any good,' muttered Jenny.

'What for?' said Mario practically. 'There's absolutely nothing we can prove, nothing at all. We haven't got any evidence and without it they're not likely to listen to us. Caldena's well known. He's liked, he's respected. They wouldn't take any notice.'

'But what about Simon himself?' asked Mike. 'Do you think he's changed at all, his behaviour, that is? I mean, does he act as though he's been having a drag?'

Mario shook his head once again so that a dark lock fell over one eye. 'You know my father's a doctor here, don't you? Well, I've already asked him about Simon and he just says that a kid like that is always changing, that he's deteriorating just a little day by day.'

'It's almost impossible to tell,' Jenny pointed out. 'I only hope he hasn't caught on to inhaling yet.'

Mike stood quite still and stared hard at them. His face was white. 'If you're right,' he said quietly, 'then we can't let Caldena get away with it. It's horrific—it's disgusting—it's . . .'

'The trouble with me,' said Jenny, 'is that I'm just no good at hiding my feelings . . .'

'You can say that again,' said Mike.

'I'm pretty sure,' she went on, 'that Caldena hasn't the slightest idea of what I suspect, but the one thing there can't be any mistake about is that I think he stinks.' She sighed. 'So, you see, there isn't a hope in hell that I'll ever find anything out unless I just stumble across it.' She eyed Mike thoughtfully. 'Now you're a much better bet.'

'Me?' Mike jabbed himself in the chest. 'I wouldn't have a clue. I wouldn't know how to go about it. I wouldn't even know what it was I was looking for.'

'You haven't got to rifle his desk or anything like that,' Jenny said impatiently. 'You'd just have to use your wits. Keep your eyes open, that sort of thing.'

'But I wouldn't fool anyone,' protested Mike. 'I'm probably the world's worst actor.'

'Who's asking you to act?' said Mario. 'You don't have to do anything. Just be natural when you meet him, act friendly, take up any invitations that come your way . . .'

'But . . .'

'Oh, all right. Forget it,' said Jenny wearily, turning away from him. 'Why should you care? You don't really know Simon or any of us, come to that. You're new to the place after all.'

Mike hesitated. The idea of spying on anyone no matter who he was made him feel positively sick but the idea of Simon innocently puffing away made him feel a great deal worse. 'Oh, okay,' he said eventually. 'I'll give it a go.' As Mario thumped him on the back and Jenny smiled up gratefully he added hastily, 'Don't go expecting too much. I probably wouldn't recognize pot if it was shoved under my nose.'

Remembering their first conversation at Xlendi, Jenny flashed an amused look at him but kept quiet as they wandered on down the road to the sea.

CHAPTER SIX

Jenny sat in the sun, book in hand, her feet in the water, staring out to sea, a disgruntled expression on her face. Far out beyond the bay James was hurtling round and round in his new boat, putting her through her paces. The sea was churned into a mountain of froth as he opened the throttle and zoomed like an angry blue-bottle in ever-tightening circles. She shook her head disapprovingly. James was just like a child, she decided. Because his own boat was in dock he simply had to find another toy to play with—and a pretty expensive toy it had turned out to be. It was a mystery to her how James kept his head above water. Still, it wasn't her business, she reminded herself, and anyway, he certainly wasn't mean as far as she was concerned. As he came a little way into the bay and waved enthusiastically at her, she dropped her eyes to her book and pretended to be absorbed in it. She certainly had no intention of waving back.

A couple of minutes later she threw the book on one side and sat there gloomily. What on earth had made her pick up such a boring one? Restlessly she splashed her feet around in the warm water. A shout from the other side of the bay made her look up and she was just in time to see Al and Nick dive in and surface. She patted the rock as they swam over and clung to the edge and grinned. 'Come and talk to me,' she said, and they hauled themselves out and sprawled at her feet.

Nick shook his head so that little spots of water fell over them all. He breathed deeply and patted his stomach. 'Am I out of condition!' he puffed. 'Another stroke and I'd have perished. I'd never have made it.'

'That, mate,' observed Al loudly, 'would have been a judgement on you. A fitting epitaph, I might say. Drowned in the drink!'

Nick wrinkled his forehead and leaned closer to Al. 'What's that?'

Al put his mouth near Nick's ear. 'Take out the plugs, O stupid one!' he shouted. As a look of comprehension crossed Nick's face and he removed two tiny earplugs, Al turned to Jenny. 'He has to wear them,' he explained. 'Ear ache. Mind you, most of him's like that. Contact lenses, false teeth, wig, screwed-on leg—he's the original phoney man.'

'Take no notice of him,' said Nick amiably. 'He only carries on like that because of his inferiority complex. He's jealous of my classic profile. See!' He turned sideways to Jenny and she took one look and burst out laughing.

'How funny!' she gasped at last. 'You don't notice from the front that your face is completely crooked.'

'So is his heart,' leered Al. 'They don't call him Black Nick for nothing.'

Nick arranged himself comfortably with his back against the rock. 'He's made it all up,' he said. 'I'm not like that at all, actually. What I like about me is that I'm ordinary. I like being ordinary. I reckon it suits me.'

'Then you'll stick out like a sore thumb on this island,' observed Jenny. 'No one's ordinary. Nearly everyone I know was halfway round the twist before they even got here. Gozo just sort of finished them off.'

'So that explains why they're all so friendly!' exclaimed Al. 'They all greet us as though we're old friends. I just thought it was our lovable natures that led to the great display of comradeship.' He looked thoughtfully at Nick and prodded him with one finger. 'Mind you, it won't do my reputation much good to be seen around with such a weakling. Look at him! Don't you think he's got something in common with a whale?'

Jenny laughed. 'Actually,' she said, 'you look like a pair of stranded dolphins.'

Al raised himself on one elbow. 'Do you mind! I take that very ill. I am only pretending to be a stranded dolphin. You ought to have realized.'

'But all dolphins are super,' Jenny pointed out. 'Super lovely and super intelligent.'

'That's a bit more like it.' Al suddenly sat up and stared out to sea. 'Look at that!' he said, a note of envy in his voice. 'That really is a beautiful launch. She looks powerful too.'

'It's James, my uncle,' said Jenny quickly, as he headed into the bay. 'Don't say anything about it. Don't mention it at all.'

James, grinning all over his red face, his hair wet with spray, puttered in. 'What do you think of that?' he shouted as soon as he was within hailing distance. 'She's a real little beauty, isn't she? Goes like a rocket.'

Jenny stared blankly at him. 'What's that?' she asked indifferently.

James's face fell. 'Didn't you see? Weren't you looking?'

'See what?' she asked innocently.

'You didn't notice!' James puffed out his cheeks and ran his hand through his hair. 'Don't you care?'

'Yes, of course.' Jenny's voice was completely flat.

'Why don't you go and do it all over again?' She swung round to Nick and Al while James, a disappointed expression on his face, idly played with the wheel. 'I'm going up to Victoria. I've got some shopping to do.'

'We'll come,' said Al eagerly and the two men jumped to their feet. 'We'll meet you by the car. It's the pale blue Triumph parked against the wall.'

'Fine, thanks. I'll just go and change. I'll meet you there in about twenty minutes.' She gave them a broad smile, nodded coolly to James, who was still sitting disconsolately in his launch, and ran up the hill.

By the time she got back to the car Al and Nick were already waiting. 'You were quick,' she said.

'Just happen to be quick-change artists,' said Al airily as he reversed the car. 'You might say that we are a compendium of all the talents. You name it—we can do it.'

'Not necessarily well,' added Nick, 'but we can do it all right.'

'Speak for yourself,' said Al, changing gear and sweeping round the corner into Victoria. 'You might be a botcher-up of jobs but not me, mate. I'm a perfectionist.' He pulled up so that Jenny could hop out. 'It's the jealous streak in him coming out again,' he said to her. 'You'd think by now he'd be used to being second best.'

Nick poked his head out of the window. 'I'm not bandying words with him when he's in his Almighty Al mood,' he said. 'It's a waste of time. I say, Jenny, we're just going to the bank and then popping into the Duke. Come and find us if you want a lift down again.'

'Thanks.'

Jenny stopped to buy a newspaper and then

drifted into the market and tried yet again to haggle over some fruit. As usual she ended up paying the original price. She stood there munching an apple. Somehow she didn't seem very good at driving a hard bargain.

Edward Albion came round the corner and peered at her in a short-sighted way. 'Ah, Jenny, good.' He dumped an old haversack on the ground, opened it carefully and fished out an envelope. 'Here you are,' he said, thrusting it into her hands. 'That's for you and James.' He pulled the strings of the bag tight, slung it on one shoulder and set off again.

Jenny glanced at it. 'Edward!' she cried, running after him. 'This isn't for us. It's for the Fiddlers.'

Edward turned round, a peevish expression on his face. 'Don't fuss, Jenny,' he said testily. 'They're all the same inside. You keep that one.' He dragged a list from his pocket and neatly ticked off James and Jenny's names.

'Can I look?' she shouted after him, but he strode on without a backward glance.

'There's no need.' Sue came out of a shop behind Jenny. 'It's one of his parties.' She pulled out her own invitation. 'Mine's addressed to Peter Lockyer.'

'I wonder if he'll miss anyone out?' asked Jenny. 'It's a hit and miss way of doing things, isn't it?'

'It won't make any difference. They'll all turn up anyway.' Sue stopped for a moment. 'Do you know how Simon is today?'

'He seemed fine. I went there early this morning. Mrs Brown told me she'd given him a terrific roasting about wandering about and she said she thought that this time he'd stay in Xlendi for a bit.'

'I wonder just how much sinks in,' said Sue thoughtfully. 'It's almost impossible to tell. He's not as stupid as some people think, I'm certain of that.'

'No, he's not,' agreed Jenny. 'What he doesn't seem to have, though, is any awareness of danger. If he did then he wouldn't drift around the way he does.'

'But his mother's absolutely right,' Sue said firmly, 'not to let him be locked up. It would be wrong for a child like that. He's just fortunate that they've brought him to live here where people don't go around sticking their fingers out at him. Look!' she pointed to Robert who was on the opposite side of the street. 'Edward's managed to trap him too. That'll really fox Robert. Ah well, Jenny, off to the butcher's. I'll see you around.'

Jenny ambled down to the Duke and sat down with her newspaper and asked for coffee. The front page was entirely devoted to the capture of Vesculdi. Suddenly she sat bolt upright. Although the police had got him all right, they hadn't managed to lay their hands on either the accomplices or the drugs. Although they had waited inside the hotel room no one had turned up and no one had made any attempt to contact him. So that was why the police had told Mike to keep his mouth shut! There they sat like spiders hoping for a fly to walk into their trap—and the fly, it seemed, wasn't fooled for a moment. Still, she thought, they'd still done pretty well to lay their hands on Vesculdi so quickly.

She put down the paper as someone sat down heavily opposite her and sighed. Robert, looking very harassed, was leaning back frowning. 'Hallo, Robert,' she said.

'Oh,' he said, half getting up. 'I didn't see you. Do you mind if I sit here?' He pulled his envelope out of his pocket and sat there turning it over and over, a baffled expression on his face. 'Very odd,' he murmured to himself. 'Very odd indeed.'

'No, it's not,' Jenny said as she poured out her coffee. 'We've got one too.' She placed hers on the table and put it next to Robert's. 'Who's yours addressed to?'

'Ralph Marquis,' Robert said in a puzzled tone. He shook his head. 'I really have no idea who he is.'

'But it doesn't matter,' explained Jenny. 'Edward's handing them around to anyone he meets. I've caught on now. He's written all the invitations and put names on them and everything but now he reckons he hasn't time to sort through them and deliver them to the right people. You know what he is about time. It's all right though. You can keep that one.'

Robert looked at her with startled eyes. 'I'm not so sure of that,' he said. 'After all, one can hardly open a letter addressed to someone else, now ...'

'It's not a letter. I thought I said. It's a party.'

'A party!' Robert sounded as if it was a new word to him.

'Yes. Everyone's coming. You've got to come, Robert. It would be a drag without you and Mike.'

'A drag?' Clearly that *was* a new word to Robert.

'Yes, a bore, you know, dull.'

'Ah! And you say Mike's invited? Of course, Edward did say something about Mike but I hardly think— after all, he's no idea of his age.'

'What's that got to do with it?' Jenny demanded. 'I'm not much older than Mike and he's asked me.'

Robert stared at her doubtfully. 'I suppose things have changed,' he said.

'You bet!' she said enthusiastically. She watched him fingering the envelope again. Poor guy, she thought, he really hasn't a clue. 'Don't worry about that,' she said at last. 'I'll see that that one gets to the right place somehow and I'll get hold of yours if

I possibly can. I'll fix it somehow even if I have to stand over Edward and force him to write you another.'

'That really is most kind of you.' Robert looked as if a great burden had been lifted from his shoulders. He poured out his own coffee and sat back again, a look of relief on his face.

Jenny looked around the Duke and saw Caldena and Mr Alberghini, their heads very close together, clearly having some sort of a confidential chat. It reminded her of her map. She plonked some sugar in her coffee and turned back to Robert. 'You know about as much as anyone else about the history of the island, don't you?' she asked.

Robert glanced up from his coffee. 'I don't know about that,' he said modestly. 'Certainly I do have a little knowledge. but there are others who are better qualified.'

'You'll know what I want to know,' Jenny declared. 'It's quite simple. What has the island been used for in the past?'

'That's rather a general question.' Robert rubbed his chin thoughtfully. 'Agriculture is the simple answer, I suppose. That and fishing. Gozo has always been regarded as a larder for Malta, you know. It's much more fertile.'

'What about the Turks? How did they see it?'

'For them it was a source of forced labour.'

'And what about the knights?'

'An outpost, a lookout, an extra base.'

'What about outsiders?'

'What exactly do you mean?'

'Has it been used by other people? What about ships?'

Robert looked at her blankly. 'Obviously it's been used by ships—throughout its history ships will have anchored here when they could get in; they'd get fresh water and supplies. It might well have been used as a base by hundreds . . .'

Jenny couldn't restrain herself any longer. 'What about the corsairs?' she asked eagerly. 'Would they have used Gozo as a loot-box, stashed their goodies away for a rainy day? After all, it was done all over the Caribbean, wasn't it? Why shouldn't it have been done in the Med? Lifting the stuff must have been kid's stuff, but finding a good crib must have been a bit more difficult.'

Robert seemed utterly exhausted by her flood of words. 'My dear Jenny,' he said. 'I must be even more out of touch than I realized. Do you know I probably understood only about one in every four words? No!' He raised his hand as she opened her mouth again. 'Once is enough. I caught the gist of it. The answer, I'm afraid, is no.' He looked at Jenny's crestfallen face. 'I'm sorry, Jenny, but it is such a remote possibility that it is almost the same as saying no. You see, the corsairs roaming the Mediterranean all had bases; great cities were founded on the wealth they brought back. Nothing would have been—er—stashed away in a loot-box as you so obviously hoped.'

'Oh.' Jenny sat still, her hopes dashed to the ground. 'I see. Well, that's that. Actually I knew all the time that there wasn't much chance that I'd got my hands on anything valuable. It was just that I sort of got carried away by the idea. It was actually having the map and . . .'

'Map? What map?' asked Robert.

'Didn't Mike tell you?' asked Jenny, surprised.

'No,' said Robert shortly. 'We seldom seem to communicate these days. Perhaps because we seem to have little time together.'

'That's nothing to do with it,' said Jenny frankly.

She ignored Robert's disapproving look and went on, 'you see, your lines of communication are blocked. You don't switch on often enough.'

'Really,' he murmured, discouragingly.

'Yes, really.' She leaned forward eagerly and fixed her eyes on him with such intensity that he began to feel a little uncomfortable. 'They *are* blocked, aren't they, Robert?'

'Well,' he murmured at last, 'maybe you're right, Jenny. Perhaps when Mike's a little older . . .'

'There you go,' said Jenny, throwing her hands in the air. 'That's what I mean. It's nothing to do with age. Can't you see? Mike's a person now. You don't have to wait till he's eighteen or twenty or something before you treat him like one.'

Feeling rather embarrassed, Robert picked up his spoon and stirred his coffee yet again. 'We—well, we seem to have very little in common, you know, Jenny. Perhaps my work . . .'

'But you don't have to go round looking for things in common,' she said patiently. 'Everything's in common—eating, sleeping, dressing—it's all common. We all do it. Why don't you just try treating Mike as though he's human?'

Robert looked up quickly, 'And you think I don't?'

Jenny bit her lips. 'It's not exactly that—or not only that,' she explained. 'It's the fact that you actually have to think about Mike especially. There's no need to get so hung-up about it. Stop thinking you have to have a different sort of relationship with him—that you have to make a special effort. Why can't you behave with him as you would with anyone else?'

Robert half-smiled at her. 'Then I wouldn't get much farther, Jenny. I happen to know that I have a reputation for being unsociable.'

'Then why not be unsociable if that's what you

want,' Jenny suggested. 'Anything's better than someone creating a phoney situation. That's the way to
really foul things up because everyone knows it's
phoney.'

'Well,' Robert said, putting down his teaspoon, 'I'll
bear it in mind, Jenny. I really think you must allow
me to buy you your coffee.'

'Of course not,' she said hastily as he got up.

Robert held up his hand again. 'I absolutely insist,'
he said firmly. 'Not only have you added a consider-
able number of words to my vocabulary but you have
opened my eyes to some extent. I can see that
another meeting or two with you might help me to
actually understand what Mike is saying apart from
anything else.'

Jenny watched him leave. 'If we all kept after
him,' she said to herself, 'he might even turn into a
real live human being one day.' Her eye fell upon
the envelope. Sighing to herself she picked it up. It
was going to be a sweat sorting that out. She tapped
it in the palm of her hand and sat there thinking for
a moment or two and then she got up and went over
to the reception desk. 'I say,' she said to the receptionist, 'you don't know a man called Ralph Marquis,
do you?'

The girl looked up from her register. 'Yes, of
course. He is staying here now. He is a friend of Mr
Albion.'

A friend of Edward Albion! Jenny grinned to
herself. If Edward hadn't been able to get the right
letter to his own friend then it certainly wasn't
surprising that he couldn't cope with all the others.
She handed the envelope over. 'Would you mind
giving him this then?'

The girl laughed and put her hand under the
counter and came up clutching a handful of identical

envelopes. 'We are becoming Mr Albion's private
post office,' she said.

'I say,' said Jenny eagerly, 'you haven't got one for
Robert Bennet by any chance, have you?'

The receptionist shuffled through them quickly. 'I
think . . .' she began, and then pulled one out of the
pile. Her face fell. 'I should have thought,' she said.
'He has just left.'

'I know.' Jenny took it from her. 'I might just
manage to catch him.' She raced out of the Duke
and leapt down the steps. Robert was still sitting
patiently in his car, his eyes glued to the mirror,
waiting for an opportunity to pull out. 'Robert!' she
shrieked. 'Robert! Wait a minute!' He looked up in
surprise as she ran down the road and thrust the
envelope in his hand. 'There you are,' she said, 'it's
all yours.'

'But I thought that you were going . . .' Robert
stopped as his eyes fell on the name scrawled on the
envelope. 'Good heavens!' he exclaimed. 'What a
remarkable young lady you are!'

Jenny really felt quite pleased with herself as she
swung down the road to Xlendi. That would teach
him not to regard all her generation as freaks and
drop-outs, she thought. Actually, she decided, Robert
really wasn't such a bad guy when you got underneath all that pompousness and he'd thawed out a
bit. Maybe if he'd had an ordinary marriage he
would have been all right. Being married to a fashion
journalist, especially a really top-flight one, must
have been a bit of a headache. It was surprising
really, that Mike had turned out all right. Of course,
he was a bit stiff. Still, going to a public school
wouldn't have helped.

Jenny wandered indoors and had a shower. Putting
on a bikini and a towelling jacket round her shoulders

she had a look inside the fridge. After a quick snack she strolled slowly out into the hot bright sun. She made her way down to the sea and sat there contentedly for a bit before plunging in. Then she climbed out again and sat on the rock, her arms clasping her knees.

Before long Freddie bounced up to her. He shook hands as she made room for him beside her. 'I have finished the practice for today,' he said, a satisfied look on his face. 'It is all over until tomorrow.'

'Do you belong to the band, then?' asked Jenny.

'Yes,' he said proudly.

'What do you play?'

Freddie beat a tattoo on the rock with his hands. 'The kettle-drum. But we still need very much more practice. It is not long to the festa now. There is still very much to do.' He shifted a little closer to Jenny and shot a quick look at the right and left of them to make sure that no one else was within earshot. 'We are making new fireworks,' he confided.

Jenny laughed. 'Old ones wouldn't be much good, now would they?'

Freddie frowned. 'You do not understand,' he said seriously. 'We are making a new sort. They will be marvellous. Fantastic. Very good.'

'I bet they will.' Jenny knew that the secret of firework making was a closely guarded one, the exact formula never openly talked about, each village literally trying to outshine the next.

'You will not tell anyone?' he asked anxiously. 'No one must know.'

'I won't say a word,' Jenny promised. She looked round the bay. There was no sign of James at all and his launch had gone. Probably showing off round Marselforn or somewhere, she thought. She suddenly realized that she hadn't seen either Mike or Mario about either. 'Freddie,' she said, 'have you seen Mike or Mario anywhere?'

'But yes.' He jumped to his feet as a distant humming grew louder and louder. He pointed out to sea. 'Look!' he said excitedly. 'There is your uncle's new boat.'

Jenny shaded her eyes from the sun and stared out across the water. James's launch was racing in, looming larger second by second as it bounded over the waves, white froth foaming around it. 'Looks like washing day,' she said crossly to herself. Suddenly she stared even harder and got to her feet to stand side by side with Freddie. Mario and Mike, balanced on either side of the cabin, stood on deck, while James's happy face beamed above the wheel. 'Well,' she said, putting her hands on her hips, 'they're nothing but a pair of rotten traitors.'

She waited until they'd tied the boat up and come ashore in the little rubber dinghy. Then, when all three of them were on dry land, she waded into them, her face stern. James's grin faded as she told him all over again what she thought of his extravagance, and the boys stood there with hang-dog expressions while she lammed into them for encouraging him. 'Not that he needs any encouraging,' she said fiercely. 'He's only interested in spending money on himself. I don't know how he's got the face to do it when there are millions of people starving . . .'

James stretched out a hand and gave her a tentative pat on the head. 'Don't be angry, Jen,' he pleaded.

Jenny knocked his hand away. '*Don't* call me . . .'

'Jen,' said the boys.

She swung round to them again. 'You ought to be ashamed of yourselves,' she said hotly. 'I've spent all day sweating around on your behalf, fixing things for you, Mike, so that you can go to Edward Albion's party and . . .' She searched her mind. What had she done for Mario? She couldn't think of anything. '. . . And keeping an eye on your interests, Mario,' she said rather grandly.

'Party!' they all said eagerly.

'Mm. Mr Albion's got the whole island in a state of utter confusion,' she said, completely forgetting her temper as she walked up to the house with them. 'And so,' she ended as Mario opened the front door for her and she disappeared through it, 'I shall have to have a new dress.'

'Yes, Jenny,' said James meekly.

CHAPTER SEVEN

Mike drifted down to Victoria on the morning of the party. He didn't quite know what to do with himself. Arthur, standing at the door of his café, greeted him affably. 'Good morning. See, we are getting ready for the festa.' He pointed across the square and Mike saw a gang of boys busily swarming round the trees stringing up loops of fairy lights. 'Of course,' Arthur went on hastily, in case Mike should be disappointed by these meagre preparations, 'it is only the start. Soon Victoria will be alight, blazing—like—' he searched his memory for a suitable comparison, 'like your blitz,' he finished up.

'I bet it'll be fantastic,' Mike said. 'But what actually gives?' He saw Arthur's blank face. 'You know, what goes on, what happens?'

'What happens?' Arthur threw his hands in the air. 'Everything happens, anything happens. That is the best part of it.'

'Ah!' said Mike. 'Sort of impromptu.'

'Impromptu?' That was a new one on Arthur. 'Yes,' he said, after a moment's thought. 'Very impromptu. Very, very impromptu. Come.' He dragged Mike inside and they sat down together at one of the marble-topped tables. 'I will tell you.' He clasped his fingers together and leaned forward. 'First, it is not one day, it is three; second, it is not all fun.' He leaned back again and stared at Mike's face. Satisfied that he was paying the proper amount of attention, he put his elbows back on the table again. 'It is very

95

serious. It is the celebration for Our Lady. We have to take her statue round all the streets of Victoria.'

'All the streets?' repeated Mike.

'Yes, every street.' He caught a glimpse of Mike's astonished face and nodded solemnly. 'Every one,' he said again. 'There is a band in front and a band behind and then in the square in front of the church she is put up for everyone to see and then we have fireworks and drinking and dancing. It is very good. Very impromptu.'

'What's impromptu then?' asked Al, as he and Nick came in together and settled down at the table with them.

'The festa,' Mike replied.

'Ah! The festa.' Nick turned an interested face to Arthur. 'What's it all about?'

'Mike will tell you,' Arthur said, getting up and going to the counter. 'I will make the tea.'

'No need to tell us,' said Al hastily, as Mike opened his mouth. 'If we've been told once we've been told a hundred times. It's all the town can talk about at the moment.' He took an envelope from inside his jacket. 'Do you know an old boy who wanders around clutching a haversack?'

'Oh,' said Mike, 'you must mean Edward Albion. I know who he is all right. I don't actually know him though.'

'Is he all right in the upper storey?' asked Nick anxiously, tapping his forehead meaningly.

'I think so. No one's ever said he's round the bend. Why?'

'Well,' said Al, in excrutiating cockney, 'we 'ave 'ere what I take to be a perfectly legitimate invite to 'is little shindig this evening . . .'

'As ever was,' interrupted Nick.

'As ever was,' repeated Al. 'The same was 'anded to

yours truly by the afore mentioned gent not 'alf an hour ago. When 'e 'as gone on 'is way, we 'appen to notice that the name on the henvelope is the name of a lady—a lady with the unlikely name of April May—so we chases after our Edward and 'e says, "Don't bother me with trifles". Now I ask you, young feller me lad, what are we to make out of that?'

'But he's been doing that all over the island.'

'Aha!' Nick waggled a finger at Mike. 'That's what we were saying. He's a loony, harmless, no doubt, but a loony just the same.'

'There's going to be a party, all right,' explained Mike. 'We're all going. Everybody's going. It's just that he reckons that as long as everybody gets an invitation it doesn't matter which one it is.'

Nick raised one black eyebrow. 'Oh, well,' he said, 'it takes all sorts, doesn't it?'

'You will go, won't you?' Mike asked, getting up.

'Fear not, dear boy,' said Al, 'we shall be there. You will find us, no doubt, in the middle of a madly gay laughing throng but we shall find time to toss you a merry little quip as you pass by.'

Nick sighed. 'He's getting above himself again. I'll try and damp him down a bit before the party,' he promised.

Mike sauntered out into the hot street and hesitated for a moment or two. At last he made up his mind and strolled round the corner and past the Band Club. A fantastic burst of music came from it and he stood on the pavement and listened. It was ear-splitting. He was just about to move on when Freddie came pelting up the street. He skidded to a halt by Mike, grabbed his hand, shook it fiercely and shot off round the corner to the side entrance, a faint cry of 'Good morning,' following him as he rushed inside.

Immediately after him, Jenny came swinging along,

97

the kaleidoscope in her hand. 'Hi, Mike,' she said.
'Have you seen Simon?'

'No. Is he in Victoria?'

'Yes,' she said positively. 'Several people have seen
him knocking around.' She linked her arm through
his. 'I've been all over the place.' She nodded up at
the trees where the fairy lights were now nestling in
the leaves. 'They're getting ready early this year,' she
said.

'When does it start?'

'Thursday.' She quickly withdrew her arm and
waved vigorously. 'There he is. Simon! Simon!' she
shouted. 'Come here!'

Startled, Simon looked round. He must have recognized Jenny but he started to run down a narrow
alley. 'That's because he's got a guilty conscience,'
Jenny said as they trotted after him. 'He knows he
mustn't come up to Victoria on his own, not after last
time.'

'But does he really understand?' asked Mike.

'Sure he does.' They came to the end of the alley
and stood staring across the wide square with the
massive church almost filling one side of it. 'He simply
can't speak very clearly because his mouth is mal-
formed. It's difficult most of the time to find out what
he's on about. After all, he doesn't know that many
words. He's not exactly quick on the uptake either but
he gets there in the end.' She suddenly spotted where
he was hiding, crouched down by the side of the flight
of steps. 'Simon!' she shouted again. 'Look what I've
got for you.'

He poked his head through a gap in the balustrade
and looked at her cautiously. She waved the kaleidoscope at him. He stared at it and then shook his head.
'Choc!' he shouted back. 'Choc!'

'It's not chocolate,' said Jenny, moving forward

slowly in case he took it into his head to run away again. 'It's a present.' He got up and took a hesitant step towards her. 'It's a kaleidoscope, Simon.' He put his great head on one side and looked enquiringly at her. 'A kaleidoscope.' She held it out. 'It makes pictures.' Simon's head wobbled and he moved back again, but this time towards the exit on the other side of the square.

'Choc, choc, choc,' he chanted insistently.

'I'll go and get him some, shall I?' said Mike.

'No. He'll just grab it and then he'll be off again. Just keep an eye on him. I won't be a tick.' Watched by the curious face of Simon she popped into a little general store and came out a couple of minutes later with the kaleidoscope covered in tinfoil. 'He's mad about silver,' she said as she twirled it in the air so that it glittered in the sunlight.

Simon's face twisted into a lop-sided grin and he lolloped towards them in his ungainly way. 'Mine.' He was already dribbling.

Jenny held it high in the air out of his reach. 'It's for a good boy,' she said sternly and Simon pointed hopefully at himself. 'Come to Xlendi with me then,' she went on. 'I'll give it to you when we get there. Then it'll be your kaleidoscope.'

Simon bounced up and down. 'Klally!' he said. 'Klally!'

'Kal-ei-do-scope,' said Jenny clearly as she led him away.

'Klally!' he cried eagerly and clutched her hand, his eyes firmly fixed on it. As they disappeared from view Mike could still hear him shouting 'Klally, klally' faintly in the distance.

The rest of the day dragged past for Mike. He mooched around Victoria a bit longer and then he went back up to Xaghra and mooched around there too. Finally he picked up a book and sat reading on the terrace until late in the afternoon when Robert came out to him.

'Mike,' he said, 'I'm afraid that somehow I've fallen behind with my schedule again. I shall have to work rather later than I'd intended.'

'Aren't you coming to the party then?'

'Of course I shall,' said Robert stiffly. 'As you well know I have already accepted the invitation. I wouldn't dream of breaking an engagement. It's just that I shall not arrive until rather late. Perhaps you'll go on ahead and apologize to Mr Albion for me.' He glanced at his watch. 'The time's getting on,' he said. 'Don't you think you'd better go and have your bath and change?'

'Sure,' said Mike. He looked doubtfully at his father's baggy trousers. 'What are you going to wear?'

'Wear?' Robert turned at the door. 'My grey suit, of course.' He looked suspiciously at Mike. 'What are you thinking of wearing?'

'Jeans and a sweater,' said Mike. Then seeing a horrified look sweep across his father's face he added hastily, 'Clean ones.'

'You must be out of your mind!' Robert exclaimed. 'You might at least do your host the courtesy of presenting yourself properly dressed.'

Mike scratched his head. 'That's what everyone wears,' he said. 'I'd look mad in anything else—unless I'd got some real gear.'

'Real gear!' his father repeated, amazed. 'Really, Mike, your language deteriorates day by day. Surely you've brought a suit with you.'

'No, I haven't,' said Mike. 'I haven't got one.'

'You haven't got a suit!' Robert looked at him in disbelief. 'Whatever does your mother think...' He pulled himself up. It was his policy to criticize his wife

as little as possible in front of his son. 'Very well,
then,' he said, going indoors. 'But do wear a collar and
tie at least.'

Collar and tie! thought Mike, as he scrubbed himself down. His father knew he was going to wear
jeans. He simply didn't have a clue. No one would
wear a collar and tie with jeans. He dried himself and
shoved them on and pulled a white sweater over his
head. Robert would just have to lump it. Nevertheless
he was quite glad that Robert didn't actually see him
leaving. He didn't actually fancy a struggle with him
just then. He tramped all the way down to Marselforn
and then turned off along the Victoria road. He
hadn't got very far before a car drew up alongside and
Al's cheerful face stuck out.

' 'Allo, 'allo, 'allo,' he said. 'Any more for the
Skylark?'

Nick opened the door. 'Hop in, mate,' he said. 'He's
in one of his nautical moods. He'll be all right as long
as you remember to touch your forelock now and
again and call him skipper.'

'Look lively now,' barked Al. 'I don't want any of
your land-lubbery ways on board my craft.' He put
the car into gear again. 'Lieutenant, issue sidearms,
prepare grappling irons, instruct the boarding party
and let me know the minute the enemy's in sight.'

Nick saluted. 'Aye, aye, sir.' He turned round to
Mike. 'We'll have to humour him, you know. He's
power mad. I think it's the moon myself. He's always
worse when it's full.'

'Stop your mutinous whispering!' roared Al. He
tooted his horn and burst into a rousing rendering of
'Rule Britannia'.

'Hey!' cried Mike. 'You've gone past it.'

Al slammed on his brakes and reversed. 'The port's
pretty crowded,' he said, surveying the array of cars

already parked there. 'Just let me work my way into that berth over there.'

'You were right, Mike,' said Nick as he rang the bell. 'I think the whole island is here.'

They stood for a few minutes waiting for someone to come to the door. Great bursts of music and laughter came from inside. Nick shuffled round a bit and then he rang again. No one answered. 'Maybe we ought to have brought the grappling irons after all,' Al remarked. He stepped back and looked up. The front of the house was beneath a terrace and he could see people moving around. He put two fingers in his mouth and let out a piercing whistle. A head poked over the top. 'Who are you?' asked a man.

Al took out the invitation and peered at it. 'April May,' he said in a deep voice.

The man laughed. 'I've been longing to meet you,' he said. 'I'm Mrs Alexis Turnbull. I'll come down and let you in.'

The door swung open and they all crowded into the little hall. The man flung open a door on the right and another on the left. 'Cloakrooms,' he said. 'Ladies' and gents'. I'll leave you to make up your own minds.'

'A nasty little problem,' said Mike. 'Just as well we are cloakless.'

They went straight through into the open court-yard. It was surrounded on three sides by arches while the fourth was a stone wall covered in flowering plants. A small fountain trickled quietly in one corner and trees shaded the central paved square. The main house seemed to be above the arches and wide terraces overlooked the courtyard. They all looked around. 'Fab-u-lous!' said Nick.

'I think we all ought to report to our Edward,' said Al. 'Let him know we're here like.'

Just getting up the stairs was difficult. The place

was packed. There were people everywhere, laughing, talking, sitting, leaning and drinking, all chattering away in a variety of languages. Halfway up Mike became conscious of the fact that he was alone. Nick and Al were mixed up in the scrum below. At last, by squeezing and wriggling, he reached the terrace and wandered along, looking hopefully into each room in turn. It was a pointless search. Edward Albion, it seemed, just hadn't got around to asking himself.

Someone thrust a glass into his hand as he passed an empty window and as he slowly sipped the punch, he stopped and bent over the wrought-iron railings. People had just started dancing in the courtyard and he saw Jenny gyrating enthusiastically, her blonde hair swinging from side to side, laughing up at a thin young man whose hair was nearly as long as her own.

Mario was dancing too, throwing himself with tremendous verve into a complicated series of steps, while an auburn-haired girl tried to keep up with him. As the music stopped he glanced up and saw Mike hanging over the railings. 'Come down,' he yelled and then, as the music started up again, he turned back to the girl.

Mike moved back to the flight of steps he'd just fought his way up. It was solidly blocked now. An elderly white-haired man was sitting quite alone on the top step, whooping and wheezing with laughter and rolling from side to side. 'Ha, ha, ha!' he roared, slapping the doorpost with the flat of his hand. 'Ha, ha, ha!' and he wiped his streaming eyes with the other. He seemed to be having such a good time that Mike didn't like to disturb him.

He went into the nearest room and found it full of depressed-looking middle-aged people. He listened to them complaining away to each other about the quality of the bread and the lack of a laundry and the

price of *The Times*. The women clacked and clicked
their teeth as one after another poured out her
grievances and the men exchanged glum looks. In
their own way, Mike thought, they seemed to be
having quite a good time too.

The couple in the next room seemed to be having a
mutually satisfying quarrel. They hurled abuse at each
other, paused to have a drink, for all the world as if it
was half-time at a football match and then launched
into the second half. Mike didn't really fancy himself
as a referee and after a short spell he got tired of
being a spectator so he went back out on to the
balcony and walked to the very end. He stood there,
looking out over the quiet moonlit countryside.
Someone came and stood by his side.

'It's very beautiful, isn't it?' Caldena said. 'I grow
more attached to Gozo every day.' He twirled his
empty glass and leaned on the balcony. 'For all that
this is the twentieth century,' he went on, 'it is—I am
not sure of the word I want—innocent, perhaps. Do
you not think so, Mike?'

Mike looked curiously at him. Could he really be
mixed up with drug running? Would a pusher carry
on like this? Surely Jenny must be wrong, he thought.
No one could be that good an actor.

'It is a strange place,' Carlo added. 'One feels that
almost anything could happen at any time and yet
that it would make not even a ripple on the surface
here.' He laughed at himself. 'I am not good at
explaining what I mean,' he said. 'My English is not
really up to it.'

'I think it's marvellous,' said Mike.

'Really?' Caldena looked pleased.

'Carlo!' called a man from below. 'Carlo! Come
down. I've got someone here who wants to meet you.
Caldena bent over the rail and raised his glass in

acknowledgement before turning back to Mike. 'We are certain to see each other again before long,' he said. He made for a little door near by, opened it and ran lightly down the stairs.

Mike gave him a couple of minutes' start and then he too went down. The stairs came out into a small candle-lit room where Sue, her hair coiled on top of her head, was standing smiling at a tall, remarkably solid-looking man. She moved towards Mike as he appeared and said, 'Mike, you haven't met Joe yet have you?'

Joe grasped Mike's hand firmly. 'We may not have met,' he said, 'but you haven't gone unnoticed. My spies have told me all about you.' Mike turned a surprised face to him.

'Don't let it bother you, Mike,' Sue said. 'Joe's an architect. His men are all over the place. He knows everything about everyone but he also keeps it all to himself,' and as she looked directly into his eyes, he laughed. 'I'll tell you what, though, we haven't met those new Englishmen yet, the ones who are looking for a place to buy. What do they do?'

As if on cue, Al swept into the room. 'Ha!' he said dramatically. 'Now is the time for me to reveal my evil self. I'm the strong right arm of the Mafia!' There was utter silence in the room. Joe went on smiling but his eyes grew cold. Sue's glass chinked as she put it down on the table.

'Oh, Lord!' said Al. 'Put my great hoof into it as usual, have I?'

'Not at all,' said Joe, after a moment. 'It is just something that we do not joke about.' He turned to Sue. 'Let's go outside, shall we?'

Mike stood there awkwardly and stuck his hands into his pockets. Al waited until Sue and Joe were out of sight and then he turned and raising an enquiring eyebrow at him. 'What gives?' he asked. 'You'd better put me in the picture, Mike, before I go blundering about again.'

'It's all about nothing, really,' stammered Mike. 'That is . . . well, what I mean is, I don't know what it's all about. Everyone seems to have got a bit edgy, ever since Vesculdi was caught.' He stopped a moment and took a long drink and chattered on nervously. It was only when he had stopped that he realized he'd told Al everything, about Caldena, the cigarettes and Simon—the lot.

Al listened intently while Mike was talking. When Mike had finished he lit a cigarette and stood watching the smoke as it curled upwards. 'It sounds,' he said quietly, as he hitched himself on to the edge of the table, 'as if you might have stumbled on something. Not that I'm saying anything about Caldena. After all, I haven't even set eyes on him, but it seems to me that you can't do any harm by keeping watch on him. It wouldn't be very clever to go round shooting your mouth off about it, though.'

'We haven't said a word to anyone else. They probably wouldn't believe us.'

Al shifted his position slightly. 'I don't suppose they would. No, what you want is something concrete to show the powers that be and you'll only get that by keeping tabs on him.'

Mike sat down and rested his elbows on the table. 'What really gets me, though, is the way he carries on about the island. He doesn't *sound* like a crook.'

Al laughed quietly. 'Who knows what a crook sounds like?'

'Do you know,' Mike went on, 'he even described Gozo as innocent.'

'Innocence,' said Al, 'is only skin deep. Just you

remember that.' He slipped off the table. 'Ah well, back to the merry-making.'

Mike looked up anxiously. 'You do think there's something in it, don't you?' and Al nodded, his face serious. Mike rubbed his hands together rather nervously. 'I suppose I shouldn't have said anything at all about Caldena,' he said uncomfortably. 'You will keep it to yourself, won't you, Al?'

Al looked him straight in the face. 'Don't worry,' he said, 'I'll be as silent as the grave. I'm always around,' he went on, 'so count on me if you want any help. It's a dirty business.'

He had almost reached the door when James poked his head round it. He stared at Al. 'I know you,' he said. 'Must have met before.'

Al shook his head and then sudden recognition spread across it. 'The launch!' he said. 'I was with Jenny when you brought her in.'

James clapped him on the back. 'We must have a get-together,' he said. 'Do you know anything about boats?' Al shook his head. 'Ah, well, never mind. A couple of hours with me and . . .'

'I'll look forward to it,' said Al quickly. 'Back later. I can see my side-kick's waving.'

James watched him go, a puzzled expression on his face. 'Funny fellow,' he said, before sauntering off. 'Didn't seem interested.'

Mike sat on for a bit, strangely relieved at having told someone about Caldena. Al had kicked around quite a bit, after all. He'd been in the army too. Underneath all that chat he was probably quite a shrewd guy.

By the time he got out into the courtyard the place was jammed with people and he gradually worked his way through. At one point he was grabbed by a woman in a long white dress and he swung around with her until someone else jerked her arm and she disappeared into the press of people again. Then he found himself dancing with Jenny. Her hair was tied back from her face now and her eyes were shining. At last she put her hand to her throat. 'I've had it,' she panted. 'I'm all in. Let's find somewhere to squat.' They made their way to a sort of pergola and sat there contentedly watching everyone else dance. 'Did your father tell you that I was completely up the spout over the map?'

'My father? I didn't even realize you'd mentioned it to him.'

Jenny laughed rather self-consciously. 'In spite of everything I'd been told I suppose that deep down I thought I'd stumbled across something pretty valuable . . .'

Mike eyed her disbelievingly. 'You don't really mean you thought it was a clue to a treasure trove or something like that?' he said.

Jenny went pink and concentrated on her feet. 'I guess I must have done. It must have been the romantic in me coming out or something like that. If I'd used my wits at all I'd have seen for myself that it just wasn't on but . . . anyway, Robert soon squashed that one.'

Mike nodded understandingly. 'He can be a bit of a squasher at times.'

'I don't know. He's not all that bad once you get to know him. He needs someone to take him in hand, that's all.'

'Don't look at me,' said Mike quickly.

The auburn-haired girl pranced into the pergola and took hold of Mike's hand. 'I've had my eye on you,' she said. 'Come and dance.'

Mike got to his feet. 'What about you?' he said to Jenny.

'Right now,' she said, 'my feet are killing me. I'm

going to take my shoes off and stick them up,' and as Mike was tugged away she kicked them off and waggled her toes about. She looked up curiously as she heard footsteps above. She hadn't known there was a terrace over her head. The feet walked up and down and Jenny stuck her head out from under the shelter and twisted her neck in an effort to see.

'I've had enough!' For all the noise going on round her Jenny could hear remarkably clearly. She settled down to enjoy it all. It sounded like the classic beginning of a good row. 'I don't like it. The place is teeming with people. Who the hell chose it?' *Not* the same thing as a good red-blooded family row, she thought. She bent forwards, her chin in her hands.

'Listen, this is for the big kill.' That was a different voice—another man's—a soft, persuasive voice. They moved again, their footsteps retreating and then returning once more.

'And another thing . . . Dwera . . .'

'Early. . . the finish tomorrow . . .'

Jenny jumped up and moved away from the shelter. She stepped back and stared up but the terrace was in darkness, the hanging vines preventing even a glimmer of moonlight from penetrating through them. A large hand grabbed hold of Jenny's and jerked her into the crowd of dancers. She tried to pull it free. 'No!' she said. 'Let me go.'

'Ha, ha, ha!' Mike's white-haired old man went purple in the face at this. 'Whoops!' He pointed a trembling finger at Jenny. 'Whoops. Ha, ha, ha!' Jenny gave him a sharp push so that he fell backwards into the surprised arms of a girl. 'Whoops!'

She turned round, raced back to the pergola and started up the stairs. Just as she reached the terrace there was the click of a switch and it was flooded with light. Caldena stood there, a faintly surprised look on his face. 'I'm sorry, Jenny,' he said. 'Had you meant to turn the light off?'

'How could I?' she snapped. 'I've only just got here.'

'I thought I saw you on it earlier,' he said. 'I thought you were using it as a private balcony.'

'What were you using it as? A conference room?'

As she flung round he put a light hand on her arm. 'Jenny,' he said. 'I'm going to surprise you.'

She stared belligerently back at him. 'And maybe I'm going to surprise you,' she retorted, clattering down the stairs. She elbowed her way through the crowds in search of Mike and Mario. 'What a nerve!' she said to herself.

CHAPTER EIGHT

Early the following morning before the sun was properly up, Mario rattled up to Mike's house and softly tooted his horn. Mike opened the door almost immediately and then shut it quietly behind him. 'Hi!' he said, squeezing in beside Jenny.

'Ouch!' she said. 'You're on my hand.'

'Sorry.' He shifted a bit. 'That better?'

'Too bad if it's not.' Mario shoved the gear into reverse and backed carefully. 'Right,' he said, 'we're off.' He cast a quick sideways look at Jenny. 'Unless you've changed your mind of course.'

'Might as well go,' she said grumpily, 'now that we've actually got this far.' She shivered a bit. 'I must have been out of my mind last night. If I'd known it was going to be so horrible this morning I wouldn't have suggested it.' She sank down deeper into her seat. 'It feels damp.'

Mike looked out at the greyish mist. 'It's not much cop,' he said. 'There's quite a few people about though, considering it's so early.'

'Farmers,' said Mario laconically.

Wisps of mist writhed around the van and seemed to close in on them. As Mario switched on the windscreen wipers, Mike rubbed hard on his window. 'It looks pretty bleak down here,' he said. 'I didn't get this far with Freddie.'

'Yes.' Mario concentrated on avoiding a pothole and the van lurched from side to side. 'I just hope it's not all a bit much for the Snorter. She deserves a bit of respect at her age.'

They drove on silently for a bit and then Mike looked at Jenny. 'What do you think it's all about? I mean, what do you think is going to happen?'

'Search me!' She twiddled with her hair. 'It all seemed such a good idea last night. I'm not so sure now.'

'Well,' said Mario, 'it can't be a bad one, can it? It can't do any harm. After all, if Caldena's interested in Dwera...'

'I wish I could be a million per cent sure it *was* Caldena,' said Jenny, moodily. 'I'm not absolutely positive it was his voice at all. I heard the words clearly enough but what with the noise and the music going on the voices seemed a bit distorted. If only he'd got a bit of an accent it would help but he speaks such perfect English...'

'Well, if he is interested in the place and we're already down here we might be able to...' Mario suddenly wrenched the wheel so sharply that they were all thrown against each other.

'Spike his guns?' said Mike.

'Spike his guns,' agreed Mario.

Jenny ran her hand through her hair. 'If it was Caldena,' she said meditatively, 'then he really played it cool.'

'He would,' Mario remarked. 'It's his style.'

They had now got to the top of a little rise and through the mist-shrouded windows Mike could just make out the tops of high cliffs a bit in front of them. 'Are we nearly there?'

'Yes.' Mario wound his way down the hill. He switched on his headlights as they suddenly ran into a solid grey wall of fog and then turned off on to a narrow track and stopped. 'Do you mind if we park here?' he said. 'She's kicking like a mule.' He switched off both the engine and the lights and they climbed out stiffly.

'Golly!' Jenny clasped her hands round herself and stamped her feet up and down. 'It's cold.'

Mario pulled off his sweater. 'Take this,' he said and she gratefully pulled it over her head. 'I'd better go first. I know this track like the back of my hand.' He set off with Jenny trailing miserably behind him and Mike bringing up the rear. The mist seemed to have got even thicker and Mike could only just make out the strange distorted shapes of the trees and bushes overhanging the gorge. The sky seemed to be lightening slightly but the sun, seen through the mist, had an odd red glow to it.

'It's a funny sort of morning,' Jenny remarked.

'It'll be clear in half an hour or so,' Mario said cheerfully. 'It'll be a scorcher later on.'

The path dipped and took an unexpected turn and Mike stumbled as the beaten earth track changed to a rocky pitted surface. He could hear the insistent swishing of water lapping against the shore. 'Are we there?' he asked, as the mist swirled round them once more.

'Nearly.' Jenny stopped and reached out for his hand. 'Hold on. It's a bit dodgy round here. Watch where you put your feet.'

Carefully they picked their way across a boulder-strewn path and then they crunched over the pebbles. The lapping of water was even louder now. 'We've reached the Inland Sea,' Jenny said. The mist whirled away for just a second and Mike found himself on the edge of an almost colourless lake, one edge of it lined with dilapidated boat-houses. Then the wispy strands of mist closed in once more and it was gone.

'Where's the sea?' asked Mike.

'Very close. You can't see the tunnel through the

cliff on the far side of the Inland Sea but if you could you'd get a glimpse of the sea beyond it. It leads straight out into deep water.'

'Can we get there any other way?'

'Sure.' Mario jerked his head sideways. 'It's over in that direction. There's a break in the cliffs and you can get right down to the water's edge.'

'What's that?' Jenny stood there listening intently. They all heard the distant putter of a boat engine.

'It's a boat,' Mike said.

'Of course it is, stupid,' said Jenny tartly. 'It sounds familiar though. Is it a luzzu, Mario?'

Mario shook his head. 'No. It sounds more like a motor-boat.'

Jenny cocked her head on one side. 'You're right, Mario,' she said after a pause. 'It isn't a luzzu. It's coming in pretty close, isn't it?'

'No, it's not,' Mike said. 'It's going away.'

'Mist does funny things to noises. A minute ago I'd have sworn it was coming in,' Mario remarked.

'Maybe it's just going round and round in circles,' Mike suggested. 'It could be quite thick out there.'

'Come on, then.' Mario turned round. 'Let's go down to the sea and find out.' He looked at Mike. 'Seen all you want to?' he asked, and they all laughed.

Although the sun was well up in the sky by this time, the mist in the valley hadn't lifted at all. The air was warmer at last although it still seemed curiously clammy. Mario led the way again. 'Watch out, Mike,' he said warningly. 'You could easily break your ankle round here. It's pitted with holes and cracks.'

Carefully they picked their way across the rough uneven surface and the sound of the sea slapping against the rocks became louder and louder. 'Shame you can't see it,' said Mario regretfully. 'It's always a fantastic colour round here.'

Jenny lurched and stumbled against Mike. 'It's weird round here. I don't like it. I never have.' She clung to Mike's arm. 'I've got goose-pimples already. Listen!' They all stood still. There were heavy stumbling footsteps near them and then the sudden crunch of pebbles. 'There's someone in front of us.'

'Behind us,' said Mario sharply.

'You're wrong!'

'Damn this fog.' Mario tried to peer through the mist. There was silence again.

Jenny shivered. 'I don't like it,' she repeated. 'Why don't we go back?'

'Go back! We can't do that.' Mario sounded disgusted at the thought. 'Anyway, it was all your idea.'

'I know it was. I don't know what got into me. It was a lousy idea.'

'Sh!' Mario lifted his hand. 'Listen!' The stumbling feet were moving again. They were quite close, slipping on the bank of pebbles round the Inland Sea. He swung round. 'It *is* behind us.'

'What are we whispering for?' asked Mike in a low voice. 'Why shouldn't there be other people round here?'

'On a morning like this?' hissed Jenny.

Mario moved forward. 'Who's there?' he asked sharply. There was silence. 'Who's there?' he said again in Maltese. They all stood there as if frozen.

'There *is* someone there,' whispered Jenny. 'I know there is. I can feel it.' A dislodged pebble suddenly started rolling down towards them, clicking sharply against others as it went and a small avalanche followed it. 'If only the mist would clear,' she muttered.

'Listen,' said Mario quietly. 'Do you think you can find your way back to the van?' She nodded. 'Then go with her, Mike, and switch on the headlights. We'll see if we can get a glimpse of whoever's prowling around.'

'Are they powerful enough?' whispered Mike. 'It's quite a distance away.'

'It's worth a try,' murmured Jenny. She was only too pleased to get away. 'What are you going to do, Mario?'

'I'm going to do a bit of prowling on my own account.'

'Right. Come on, Mike.'

Together, stepping as cautiously as possible, they made their way back to the van. 'Here we are,' Mike hissed. 'I'll switch on while you keep your eyes skinned.'

'And now what are we whispering for?' she said. 'There's no one up here at all. Look, wait a minute. I'm going to get up a bit above you. I'll get a better view from there. If there's anything to be seen I'll stand a better chance of spotting it. Give me a couple of minutes. I'll give you a shout when I'm ready.' Mike heard her scrambling about behind him as he fumbled with the key and put his hand on the light switch and waited. 'Right!' she yelled. 'Now!'

As he pressed it a beam of light shot out from the headlights piercing the mist and penetrating far down into the valley. At the same moment a boat engine roared and whined and the sound of churning water came faintly up to them. A brilliant spotlight cut through the damp grey curtain of fog and was just as suddenly cut off. A strange flickering could be seen and then it reappeared, dancing over the waters of the Inland Sea. In that same moment, as if by magic, the sea mist rolled away, parted as if by a knife, and the sparkling sun shone down. As the launch circled the Inland Sea a figure on deck hurled a glittering packet into the shadows, and then it shot back into the shelter of the tunnel.

From behind a boat-house, Simon's grotesque shape

emerged. He waded out into the water and picked the
packet up, holding it closely to his chest. There was
the roar of yet another powerful engine behind Mike
and he turned sharply to see a large car hurtling down
the twisting path, lurching wildly from side to side. At
the sound of the engine Simon's head jerked like a
puppet's from side to side. Still clutching his shining
bundle he began to run to the far end of the shingle
where he clambered clumsily up an outcrop of rock
and then disappeared from view.

The car screeched to a halt and two men leapt out
and began to run across the pebbles while the third
busily reversed the car. Mario rushed into the path of
the men, blocking their way. Suddenly one of them hit
him hard in the stomach and he slipped and fell and
lay there, his arms clasped tightly across himself.

'Mario!' screamed Jenny. 'Mike!'

Mike was already moving before she spoke. He ran
furiously down the hill, heedless of obstacles, and
slithered up over the shingle to Mario who, still bent
double, was slowly climbing to his feet. By this time
the men had reached the rock and Jenny could hear
their voices calling to each other as they slipped down
the other side of it.

Jenny, still on her ledge, saw it all as if it was a
play. Far in the distance Simon was lurching along the
ridge of a rock. She put her hands to her mouth.
There was an almost sheer drop on the other side. His
head disappeared from view as he plunged over and
for a moment there was silence again. The two men
reappeared and scrambled up to the top of the ridge
and stood there together looking down. They turned
quickly as Mike and Mario stumbled towards them.
Easily they dodged past and ran down the slope again
and headed for the car, while the boys slithered round
once more to chase them.

Jenny jumped off her ledge and raced towards the car too. She hadn't the faintest idea of what she could do but she just couldn't stand around any longer. She pelted down the hill but before she was even within twenty yards of the car, the men had piled in and the driver was racing off again. As it shot past she caught a quick glimpse of dark hair and tanned faces and then it was gone.

From behind came the familiar crunching of pebbles and shingle as Mike and Mario returned. Mario was still breathing hard and massaging his stomach while Mike, very pink-faced, walked slowly by his side.

'Didn't get anywhere near them,' said Mike bitterly.

'It was my fault really,' gasped Mario, collapsing on to the ground. 'If Mike hadn't stopped to help me he might just have got one of them.'

'Just as well,' said Jenny soberly. 'They looked a tough pair and the one in the car would have joined in too.' She looked down at Mario. 'Are you really all right?' she asked anxiously.

'Just a fist in the guts,' he said, breathing deeply. 'Might have been worse.'

Suddenly she frowned. 'Simon. Was he okay?'

'Simon?'

'He went over the ridge just before you got there.'

'But there's nothing on the other side—just a drop.' Mario sat up again.

'We'd better look.' Jenny's face was concerned.

'There's no need.' Mike pointed to the distant cliff. They all stared at Simon, his figure clearly outlined against the blue sky.

'How on earth did he get up there?' asked Jenny in amazement.

Mario shook his head. 'Can't imagine. He must have nine lives, that's all I can think.'

Jenny squatted down beside him. 'What was all that about?' she asked.

'Easy,' said Mario. 'The boat was outside waiting for a signal, we flashed our headlights, they thought that was what they had been waiting for, zoomed in, dropped the bundle, zoomed out and Simon grabbed it.'

'So the car was really there for the pick-up,' said Mike thoughtfully.

'Then the strong-arm boys rushed in and hoofed it after Simon but he got clear.' Jenny looked at the boys. 'Who were those men? Did you recognize them?'

Mario shook his head so that a lock of hair fell over one eye. 'Never seen them before,' he said. 'They were strangers to me.'

Jenny cupped her chin in her hand. 'I'll tell you one thing though. That was Caldena's car.'

The boys stared at her. 'Caldena's car!' Mike repeated. 'Are you sure?'

'Yes,' she said positively.

'Look,' said Mario, struggling to his feet, 'let's go to the police. They really ought to know what's been going on.'

'What do you think was in the package that Simon snaffled?' asked Mike as they walked slowly up the hill to the car.

'Haven't a clue,' said Jenny. 'But whatever it was we ought to get it off him otherwise ...' Her face went pale and she came to a halt. 'They must want it pretty badly, mustn't they? After all it was an elaborate enough set-up.' She looked anxiously at the boys. 'Simon might get hurt,' she said.

Mike and Mario exchanged worried looks. 'She's right,' Mike said. 'You don't fix something like this for peanuts.'

'No, you don't,' Mario said quietly.

They reached the van in silence and climbed in together. Mario switched on. The engine turned over slowly and reluctantly. He pulled out the choke. 'Must be cold,' he said, and tried again. The engine spluttered for a moment and then went dead. Mario sat there fuming. 'It's the blasted battery,' he said angrily. 'I should never have left the headlights on all that time. I knew it was practically flat.'

They went on sitting there mournfully. 'What are we going to do?' asked Jenny at last.

'Walk,' he said grimly, getting out.

The early morning might have been misty and cold but by now it was blazing hot. They stomped along in silence, occasionally rubbing their arms over their sweating faces. The road was extraordinarily empty. Nothing came down or went up it and they plodded on, panting more and more loudly every time they reached yet another hill.

Jenny suddenly stopped. 'I'm not walking any further,' she said rebelliously.

'Oh, come on, Jenny,' said Mario wearily. 'Don't be so wet.'

She pushed her limp hair back off her face. 'You can do what you like,' she said defiantly. 'I'm staying here. You can send a rescue party out later for me. I'm whacked.'

'So am I,' sighed Mike, leaning up against a convenient tree.

'What's the point of going on,' she continued. 'Someone will come past sooner or later. You know they will.'

'Of course I do,' snapped Mario. 'I'm not stupid. It's just that I think we ought to get to the police as soon as possible. They might stop them getting off the island . . .'

'You must be joking! Don't you realize what time it is? Both the early ferries will have gone by now so if they were going to leave they'll have left. There isn't a hope in hell of stopping them now. They'll be well away.'

Mario looked down at his watch. 'I guess you're right,' he said.

'You don't think they'd hang around then?' asked Mike.

'Not a chance,' said Mario with absolute certainty. 'After all, I got a very good look at the one who thumped me and he knew I did. No, they'll clear out all right.' He sighed and leaned up against the other side of Mike's tree.

There was the rumble of an engine in the distance and they all looked up hopefully. Mike straightened up. 'It's a lorry,' he said. As it trundled along the road towards them, Jenny danced around in the road waving her arms about while Mike and Mario stood sideways, their thumbs in the classic autostop position.

'Hi!' The driver pulled up and leaned his head out of the cab. 'You want a lift?'

'Please,' said Mike.

'Could you drop us off at Santa Lucija?' asked Mario.

'Santa Lucija?' He shook his head. 'I just come from there. You wait. I take this and come back.'

'How long?' asked Mario.

He spread his arms. 'Who knows? One hour maybe. Maybe more.'

Jenny hopped on to the step and hauled herself up so that her blonde head was just under his nose. 'Please!' she said.

'Sure.' He grinned at her. 'You climb over and sit here.' He patted the seat next to him. He looked down at the boys. 'Very sorry,' he said. 'No more room in. You must go behind.'

'Fine, thanks.' Mario grinned back at him. The grin faded as he and Mike ran round to the rear and the smell of pig-swill hit them. They looked at each other. 'After you,' said Mario grimly.

Jenny walked round to meet them when the driver dropped them just outside Victoria. Her fingers flew to her nose and she pinched it tightly. 'Phew! You stink! Honestly, you'll have to walk on the other side of the road. I can't bear it.'

They gave despondent waves to the driver as he turned round and, feeling like lepers, followed Jenny through the streets, the unmistakable whiff of pig-swill enveloping them like a cloud. Muttering people stepped on one side to let them pass and a child or two skipped along by their side, giggling and shouting. Their faces grim, they tramped along until they reached the police station.

Jenny turned round. 'You'd better wait outside,' she said. 'I'll go and see the Inspector first. I'll tell him you smell like sewers so if he wants to talk to you he'll probably come outside. If he doesn't he'll have to have his office fumigated afterwards.' She ran lightly up the steps and went in. Within seconds she was out again, her face worried. '*He's* in there,' she said.

'Who?'

She ran down to them. 'Caldena.'

'Caldena!'

'Yes.' She bit her lip. 'What do you think he's doing?'

'No idea.' Mario tugged thoughtfully at one ear. 'That is—well, he must be spinning them some yarn. He must have heard we spotted his car. That must be it.'

Mike thought for a moment. 'You don't suppose,' he said hesitantly, 'that the police could be in on it?'

'In on what?' asked Jenny.

'Well, you know,' he said awkwardly.

Mario's brows creased. 'That's ridiculous!' he snapped. 'It's impossible!'

'Is it?' Jenny regarded him seriously.

'Of course it is. I know them. My father knows them all. Everybody knows them. If they were . . .' he hesitated, unsure of the right word.

'Corrupt,' said Mike flatly.

'Yes, corrupt, then everyone would know.' His face had become pink and his eyes were angry.

'Sorry.' Jenny stared at her feet. 'I ought to have known better than to dare to criticize the . . .'

'Oh, don't be stupid! There's no need to get on your high horse.'

'*Me* on *my* high horse! I like that.' Jenny's blue eyes were as angry as his brown ones. 'It's simply that you can't face the fact that it's just on the cards that your perfect little island might not be quite so perfect after all!'

'Shut up the pair of you!' said Mike loudly. 'If you've got to squabble like school kids go and do it somewhere else. You've got half of Victoria looking at you.'

Startled, they swung round. Mike was quite right. They had got a small audience. Quite a number of kids were hanging around and one or two people were staring at them with amused eyes. Standing at the back of the crowd, a faint smile on his face, was Caldena. He caught sight of Mike looking at him and he beckoned. Mike gave the others a surprised look and went forward a yard or two. The crowd parted like magic and Mike suddenly became aware again of the horrible smell following him around. 'I'd

123

better not come too close,' he said, and Caldena nodded understandingly.

'I was hoping to see you,' he said. 'I have taken the liberty of asking James if I might borrow his new launch the day after tomorrow. I thought you might like to come out for a trip with me.'

Mike looked back. 'We can't,' Mario said hastily. 'Jenny and I have promised to spend the day helping Richard with his car.' Mike frowned. It was the first he had heard of it.

'What a pity.' Caldena looked really disappointed. 'I had thought it rather a good idea.'

'Doesn't James mind lending you his boat?' Jenny said coolly. 'He's usually fussy about the people he lends things to.'

'No.' Caldena's face was puzzled. 'He knows that I am careful. I have sailed with him before. We went to Sicily and to North Africa together last year.' He returned to Mike. 'You will be on your own anyway,' he said persuasively, 'so why don't you come. I don't think you will find it too dull.'

Mike stood there silently for a moment or two and then he looked into Caldena's face. 'Yes,' he said. 'Yes, I'd like to.'

'Good. Then that is settled. I shall not be able to pick you up, I am afraid. My car was stolen this morning. I have just been to report it to the police.' Jenny gave Mario a sharp nudge. 'It is very curious, however, for they have already found it at . . .'

'Don't tell me,' said Jenny drily. 'It was at the ferry all the time.'

Startled, he looked hard at her. 'My dear Jenny,' he said, 'how very clever of you. How did you guess?'

'Easy. Someone must have been in a hurry.'

'But why did they not take it across to Malta?'

'Perhaps they didn't want to inconvenience you,' she said, her voice as smooth as silk.

'Inconvenience me? I don't know what you mean.' Caldena frowned.

'A friend would know that you might want it later on, wouldn't he?'

Caldena shook his head. 'I hardly think a friend would take it without my permission.'

She tossed her head. 'That's just what I meant,' she said, a triumphant little smile on her lips, and walked away with Mario.

'I cannot think why Jenny always sounds so hostile now,' said Caldena to Mike. 'I just do not understand why she has changed.'

'It's just the way she puts things,' said Mike quickly. 'She doesn't mean half the things she says.'

Caldena put a heavy hand on his shoulder. 'Perhaps it is the way girls are these days,' he said. 'I must try to keep in touch a little more.' He smiled in a friendly way. 'You haven't been to the Blue Lagoon yet, have you? Believe me, it's well worth a visit. I'll meet you down at Xlendi at about eleven in case we do not happen to meet tomorrow.'

'Fine.' Mike gave him a brief smile and hurried after Jenny and Mario. He didn't have to go far. They had halted just round the corner.

'You must be round the twist, Mike,' Jenny said. 'I wouldn't go anywhere with him, certainly not in a boat, not after this morning.'

'Neither would I,' agreed Mario. 'I don't trust him an inch. You see, I was right. He'd already got in with his story first. Fat lot of use it would be for us to go to the police now. He's cut the ground from under our feet.'

'Look here,' said Jenny. 'We ought to find Simon

and see what he's done with that packet. We can't let him wander around the island on his own now.'

Mario hesitated. 'I wonder if we should go to the police after all, and just miss out the bit about Caldena. They could search for Simon too.'

'No. Let's have a go on our own first. They'll scare the living daylights out of Simon. You know what he's like. He might try to tell us but he won't utter a word to anybody else.'

'I think you're probably right,' said Mike.

'Well, okay,' agreed Mario reluctantly, 'but . . .'

Jenny suddenly moved away from them. 'You'd better get cleaned up first,' she said, wrinkling up her nose. 'The pig-swill's going sour.'

CHAPTER NINE

By the time they'd all had baths and changed and had
something to eat it was well after three. Jenny looked
out at the dazzling sunshine. 'I'm still whacked,' she
declared. 'I can hardly bear to trudge off again.'

Mario pushed his chair back. 'It's a pity about the
Snorter,' he said. 'Victor's going to tow it back for me
and recharge the battery but I shan't be able to have
her again until tomorrow.'

Reluctantly they all got to their feet. 'What shall
we do?' asked Mike. 'I mean, what's the best way to
organize a search. Shall we all split up or stick
together?'

'Split up, I think,' said Mario. 'Jenny can go to his
house since that's the most likely place for him to be
and you and I can look around Victoria. I'll go up to
the Citadel and do the top part of the town and you
can work your way up. Suppose we all meet back
at the Duke at about six. If we haven't laid our hands
on him by that time we can decide then what to do
about it.'

Jenny put her hands on her hips and frowned.
'That's all very well for you two,' she said indignantly,
'but it's miles down to Xlendi and if I've got to come
all the way up again I'll die of exhaustion on the way.
I'll never make it.'

'Yes you will,' cried Mike, and he leapt in one stride
from the café to the road and waved wildly at Al and
Nick who were cruising along very slowly. 'Are you
doing anything much?' he asked.

'Just driving round and round actually,' said Nick. 'We've been to look at a farmhouse but it wasn't really big enough. You don't happen to know of anything, do you?'

Mike ignored this. 'Could you give Jenny a lift down to Xlendi and back?'

'It'll be a pleasure,' said Al. 'A pleasure for us, that is. I'm not so sure about Jenny. She'll have to sit very close to him, you see.'

Mike turned round to Mario and Jenny. 'That's all right then. Couldn't we all meet a little earlier though? Like five or five-fifteen?'

'Okay,' said Jenny, tumbling into the back of the car. 'Thanks,' she said to Al as he pulled out. 'What a day!'

'I must say you look as if you've had quite a time,' said Nick. 'Why don't you stay down in Xlendi? We could bring a message up to the others for you.'

'No,' she said firmly. 'I'd better do it myself.'

'Where are we going?' asked Al as he drove down the Xlendi road.

'Simon's house. The Browns'. It's almost the last house on the cliff top.'

Al edged carefully round the corner and drove sedately up the hill. 'Here!' said Jenny, but he drove rather faster past it, lurched off the road and stopped with a jolt just short of the cliff edge. 'Just thought I'd turn . . .' he began and then he caught sight of Jenny in his mirror. He looked back at her. She was huddled up in the corner, shaking, her hands covering her eyes. 'What's up?' he asked.

'Sorry.' Jenny's voice was trembling. 'I—I thought we were going right over.'

'No, no, no, you foolish girl,' he said. 'Your Uncle Al was just going to do a rather neat three-point turn. Look, you hop out and pop into Simon's and then you won't have to watch.' He reached back and swung the door open. Jenny put one foot outside and then withdrew it quickly. 'I can't,' she said, her face white. 'I can't.'

Al frowned. 'You can get along there easily enough. There's at least a couple of feet.'

'No, I can't,' she whispered. 'I can't. It's heights. I'm petrified by them. I'm like a rabbit. I can't move.'

Nick patted her hand reassuringly. 'Leap out this side then,' he said. 'There's stacks more room on this side.'

Al slipped out of his seat and hurried round to the other side and opened the door for her. 'Come on,' he said, 'hang on to me. It's as safe as houses.'

Jenny moved across and eyed the ground and then she swung her legs out. 'If only you knew,' she said, her voice rather more controlled now, 'what a fool I feel.'

'I can guess,' said Al cheerfully. 'I feel one most of the time.'

She ran up the steps and knocked at the door. 'Mrs Brown,' she called. 'It's me. It's Jenny.'

Mrs Brown, her plump face looking rather worried, hurried to the door, a cup in her hand. 'Jenny,' she said thankfully. 'I am glad to see you. You haven't seen Simon, I suppose? He's been out for hours. I don't even know what time he left the house but when his father got up at half past seven he'd already gone. I've been getting more and more bothered as the time's gone on. He is getting a naughty boy.' She suddenly noticed the cup she was still holding. 'Come and have a cup of tea with me,' she suggested.

Jenny hovered on the doorstep. She looked back at Nick and Al. 'I don't think I can,' she began, 'you see . . .' She glanced at Mrs Brown's anxious face. 'Wait a minute,' she said and darted back to the car.

'That's all right then,' she said as she returned.
'They'll wait down at St Patrick's for me.'

Mrs Brown led the way into the neat, cool living-
room and stood by the window twisting her wedding
ring round and round. 'Then you haven't seen him?'
she said.

'Yes, but that was ages ago,' answered Jenny. She
wondered for a second whether to say anything about
what had happened at Dwera and then decided
against it. After all, he'd certainly got away from
there. There wasn't much point in worrying Mrs
Brown any more than she already was. After all, for
all they knew Simon was happily playing with the
water at Marselforn or somewhere. The men who had
been chasing him had clearly left the island so he was
probably safe enough.

'I just don't know what to do,' Mrs Brown said.
'My husband's had to go to Malta on business and I
really don't know what to do for the best. The last
time he disappeared like this we had the whole of the
police force out searching for him and they found him
later on sleeping in a church. They were very nice
about it but I must say I felt very foolish.'

'I remember James telling me about it,' said Jenny.
'That was during a festa too, wasn't it?'

'Yes. The Xaghra one. He loves those images, you
know, the ones they take around the town. I think it's
the gold and silver and tinsel that attracts him so
much. He just loves that old kaleidoscope you gave
him and I'm sure it's because of the tinfoil. He hasn't
learned to look through it but he takes it everywhere
he goes.'

Jenny moved towards the door. 'At least you've
given me one idea,' she said. 'We can look in all the
churches for you. Mike and Mario are up in Victoria
keeping an eye open for him. If we haven't found him

by the time it's dark we'll come straight down or telephone you or something and then you can decide if you want to get on to the police.'

'Would you?' Mrs Brown brightened up. 'That would be kind. Richard should be back by then. He'll be on the seven thirty ferry. He'll know what's best.'

'He'll know what's best!' Jenny repeated scornfully to herself as she went down to find Al and Nick again. She liked Mrs Brown well enough and admired her for keeping Simon instead of letting him go into an institution, which was what a lot of mothers might have done in her place. But she simply didn't have any patience with women who couldn't or wouldn't know how to make up their own minds.

'All right?' Nick had strolled up to meet her.

Jenny tossed her hair back. 'He's not at home,' she said. 'We'll just have to look round Victoria for him.'

'What do you want him for?' asked Al curiously.

'Nothing much. We saw him ages ago near Dwera. We just wondered where he'd got to.' For some reason she didn't feel much like discussing the morning's events with them. 'It's a lonely and dangerous bit down there, you know. If he slipped and broke his leg or something he might not be found for ages.'

'Dwera.' Nick turned to Al. 'We haven't been that way yet, have we?'

'Nope.' Al pulled a piece of paper out of his pocket. It was a scrawled list of properties. None of the houses on that side of the island had been crossed out. 'We've been tearing Nadur apart this afternoon. Nice little village. Can't believe there's nothing for sale. They must be holding out on us.'

'Why don't we give it a go now?' Nick suggested. 'There's still enough time to look at a couple of places.'

'You might have a look for him then,' said Jenny as they got back into the car. 'When we last saw him he was heading for San Laurenz.'

'San Laurenz,' Al repeated as he drove into Victoria. 'Anything to oblige. Where else do you think he might head for though? Has he got any favourite spots? It wouldn't take us long to cover them in the car.'

'Well,' Jenny sucked her underlip thoughtfully. 'At one time he was always playing around the salt pans and there was another spell when he was stuck on Mgarr—but it doesn't really mean anything.'

'Never mind. I must say I'd like to find him,' said Al.

'So would I,' said Jenny.

She got out of the car and went into the square where garlands were being strung across the street. She looked thoughtfully at the church and ran up the steps, feeling in her jeans' pockets. Bother! she thought. She hadn't got either a scarf or a handkerchief. She really couldn't go in without something to put on her head. She put her nose round the door. The inside of the church was transformed. The walls were draped in rich velvets and tapestries and everything blazed with light. The church's treasures were lined up against one wall ready to be displayed and the gold and silver shone brilliantly. She suddenly saw Freddie, his arms full of candlesticks, hurrying down the aisle. 'Freddie,' she hissed.

He looked up and smiled. Then he carefully put his load down and came out to her. 'Good afternoon,' he said, shaking hands.

'Freddie, have you seen Simon today?'

'Sure.'

'How long ago?' she asked urgently.

He rubbed his head. 'It was after the practice,' he said, 'and I came straight down here. It must have been about eleven or twelve, I think.'

Jenny sighed with relief. 'Here!' she exclaimed. 'Well, that's something.'

Freddie shifted around awkwardly. 'Jenny,' he said, examining his feet, 'it is not for me to say, but I do not think that Simon should come here to the church alone, not until after the festa.'

'No?' She was astonished.

'No. He touches everything. He cannot keep his hands away and they are always dirty. I know,' he went on earnestly, 'that it is not his fault, but everything must always be cleaned again and today he knocked over the candlesticks near Our Lady, those near her feet, and there was almost a fire. You know we clothe her in a blue and silver dress?' Jenny nodded. 'The flames nearly caught it, but luckily we heard Simon shout and then when we were cleaning all over again we found that he had wrapped sellotape all over the candlesticks and on her feet.'

'Sellotape!' cried Jenny incredulously. 'What on earth was he doing with sellotape?'

'Who knows?' Freddie spread his hands wide and then tapped his head. 'I do not know what goes on up there.'

'Neither do I, Freddie.' Jenny smiled gratefully at him. 'I'll tell his mother and we'll all try to head him away from the church.'

'But wait.' He tapped her on the back and, as she turned again, he looked at her with dark serious eyes. 'There is one more thing. I think he has taken away a little silver box with a lid. It is certainly missing. Of course, he does not know what he has done and I know his mother or whoever finds it will bring it back but . . .' his voice trailed away.

'That's really serious,' said Jenny. 'I wonder what came over him? I mean, he's never taken anything before.'

'It would be good,' said Freddie, 'if the box came back before anyone else noticed it was missing. It is a very little box. Perhaps . . .'

'You mean you haven't told anyone else?' Jenny exclaimed. He shook his head. 'You're a really good guy, Freddie. I'll tell the others straight away. We'll see if we can lay our hands on it quickly for you.'

She rushed back to the Duke and found Mario and Mike had already beaten her to it and were sitting there having coffee. 'Found anything out?' asked Mike.

'Yes.' She ran through her story quickly.

'Sellotape and a silver box!' cried Mario. 'What an extraordinary combination.'

Mike looked baffled. 'What on earth could you do with a silver box and sellotape?' he asked. 'Just stick one up with the other, I suppose.'

'Or put one inside the other,' Mario suggested.

'They might not have anything to do with each other,' Jenny pointed out. 'He might have just fancied them.' She looked at each of the boys in turn. 'You haven't found out anything, I suppose?'

'Mario has. His news is a bit later than yours. Simon was seen heading up the Gharb road, chattering away to himself, and clutching his old klally.'

'How far up the Gharb road?'

'Not far,' said Mario. 'Just past the convent. One of Joe's men noticed him. He was gabbling away and slashing the air with what the man called a silver stick.'

'Is it worth slogging all the way out there?' asked Jenny. 'Suppose he got all the way to Gharb.'

'I just don't know,' Mario said.

They sat there silently for quite a long time and then the sudden chiming of a bell made Mike look up sharply. 'It's six!' he exclaimed. 'You know how quickly it gets dark. We can't just sit here. We ought to do something.'

Jenny pushed herself up. 'Let's try the Gharb road,' she said with sudden resolution. 'The ferry gets in at seven thirty and Mrs Brown won't make up her mind to do anything about telling the police until her husband gets back so that gives us the best part of a couple of hours.'

As they approached the crossroads Jenny suddenly said, 'You know, I can understand the silver box bit but the sellotape sticks in my throat. I can't imagine where he got it.' They turned the corner. 'You don't think that package was full of it, do you?' She suddenly giggled at herself. 'Can't you see it in the headlines? The sellotape smuggling case!'

Neither of the boys spoke. They simply moved a little faster, Mario's face looking rather more worried than it had.

Mike shot a look at him. 'Are you thinking . . .?'

'Yes,' he said curtly.

Jenny hadn't noticed, she was still laughing weakly to herself.

As the sun got lower in the sky they all increased their pace once again. Once they were out of Victoria there weren't a great number of buildings at all and it wasn't long before the convent came in sight. 'Let's knock at every door,' said Mario. 'If anyone had been in their garden or looking out of their window they might have seen him pass by.'

'You could hardly miss him,' Jenny said soberly.

At one house after another people shook their heads and their feeling of elation rapidly dropped away. It began to get darker and one or two stars glimmered faintly in the dusky sky, Mario looked up. 'Another half hour,' he said firmly.

It was Mike who knocked at the right door. The others, standing by the gate, saw the nodding and pointing going on. He trotted back, his face beaming. 'It was ages ago,' he said, 'but they spotted him all right. He wandered off this road and went up that track opposite.'

'But there's nothing up there!' exclaimed Jenny.

'Yes, there is,' said Mario. 'It goes past that old windmill and some ruined farm buildings and comes out on the Marselforn road. Come on.' He strode off and the other two hurried to catch up with him. It was hard going and the surface of the track got rougher and rougher and more and more dusty as soon as they were out of sight of the road.

'This is a bit of a wild-goose chase if you ask me,' Jenny remarked as they came to the windmill.

'I'm afraid,' Mario said, 'that I think we should do a quick inspection of this place.'

Jenny's mouth went down. 'Must we?' she said. 'It smells. It looks disgusting too.'

'You don't have to come,' said Mike. 'It's not very large. Mario can do downstairs and I'll do up.'

It didn't take Mario very long and he came out covered in dirt and cobwebs. 'You did the right thing, Jenny,' he said.

There was a sudden shout from Mike and they both looked up. He was hanging out of a window pointing. 'What is it?' Mario called. 'Do you need me?'

'No. There's nothing here, but I can see something silvery lying by the door to those old farm buildings. It's a kind of silver stick, I think.'

Jenny set off. 'It's klally,' she said. 'I bet it is.' Mike ran down the stairs and hurried after them. She reached the door just ahead of Mario and pushed it open and stepped into the dim little room. Her hand went to her mouth and her eyes opened wide. She clutched the door as the blood drained from her face.

Simon lay there perfectly still. His eyes were wide open but they were glazed. Blood had dried on his arms and his face was badly scratched. Saliva had trickled from his mouth on to his chin and down his neck. Round his lower lip there was a caked white blotch, for all the world as if he had tried to be sick and failed.

'He's dead!' Jenny looked at the motionless body and the unseeing eyes. 'He's dead!'

Mike, a look of horror in his face, stood close to Jenny and clutched her hand while Mario swiftly knelt by Simon and tried to find his pulse. 'Quickly, Jenny,' he said. 'Get back to the road. Find a telephone and get help.'

Mike pushed her roughly towards the door. 'Do what he says. Hurry!'

Jenny fled back down the track and staggered at last on to the main road. A white car was speeding along, its sidelights shining in the dusk. Recklessly she stepped into the road and waved her arm. The car slowed down and stopped. Joe put his head out and then he smiled. 'Jenny!' he said. His face changed as she stumbled towards him on sagging legs. 'What is it?'

She began to sob. 'Simon,' she cried, pointing down the lane. 'He's hurt—or he's . . . please, Joe . . .'

Joe indicated the house across the road. 'Get them to telephone Dr Timaldi. Wait there.' Expertly he reversed and shot off up the track.

Exhausted, Jenny stumbled across the road and hammered on the door. A neatly dressed woman opened it, smiling, and then her face changed. She grasped Jenny's elbow and propelled her inside. 'An accident?' she asked.

'No—yes, I don't know.' Jenny couldn't think coherently. 'Please, get Dr Timaldi. His son is with Simon . . .' Her legs trembled violently, they wouldn't support her any longer and she sank into a chair by the window and sat slumped there while the woman went directly to the telephone and spoke urgently into it. A few minutes later she came back into the room, a glass in her hand. 'Drink this.'

Jenny sipped at the liquid and coughed sharply. It was brandy. 'I can't.' Tears came into her eyes again and she brushed them away with the back of her hand.

'One more sip,' the woman said coaxingly and Jenny obediently swallowed a little more. 'Are you feeling better?' Jenny swallowed hard and nodded. 'Good. Dr Timaldi is on his way. What was it? What has happened?'

The colour was beginning to come back into Jenny's face. She sat a little straighter. 'I don't know what's happened. That boy—the one you saw . . .'

'Ah! The one with the stick.'

Jenny shook her head. 'Yes . . . he's ill, there's some blood—but his eyes. He might be . . .' She put her hand to her head and rested her elbow on the arm of the chair trying to keep back the tears that sprang into her eyes once again. The woman sat with her, watching anxiously, her hand smoothing down Jenny's hair, glancing every few minutes out of the window until Dr Timaldi's car arrived and turned up the lane.

Jenny sat there staring as it grew darker and darker. Eventually the car reappeared, Dr Timaldi driving it, his face grim, while Joe sat in the back clasping a blanket-covered bundle in his arms. Carefully the car turned into the main road and drove off. Jenny sat

on, her eyes straining into the gathering darkness. At
last she could just make out the figures of the two boys
as they came slowly down the rough track. Something
glittered in Mike's hand as he swung it to and fro.
Jenny turned to the woman. 'Thank you,' she said
quietly. 'There are my friends. Thank you for staying
with me.'

The woman got up too. 'You may stay,' she said.
'You may all stay here.'

Jenny shook her head. 'Thank you,' she said again
and as the woman opened the door she gave her a
quick little smile and went down the path.

Mario and Mike saw her coming and stood still.
They both looked utterly exhausted, their strained
white faces barely visible now. Jenny held out her hand
and Mike put the kaleidoscope into it. She stared
down. 'What was it?' she asked. 'What's happened to
him?'

Mike kicked a stone and Mario looked over her
shoulder. 'Later,' he said. 'Joe is here.'

Joe drew up in Dr Timaldi's car. He got out and
put an arm round Jenny's shoulders. 'He's in the
convent hospital,' he said. 'Your father is still with
him, Mario.' He handed Mario the car keys. 'Do you
feel capable of driving back to the convent? Then
take it back for your father. Go with him, Mike. I'll
pick you up in a few minutes when I come past and
drive you all home,' He glanced down at the silent
little group. 'Perhaps we'll stop at the Duke on the
way and have some coffee. You look as if you can all
do with some.'

Mike and Mario climbed silently into the car and
drove away while Joe, his arm still round Jenny's
shoulders, guided her along the lane. She forced her
tired legs along, her mind, for the moment, a total
blank. Joe's car glowed white in the dark. He got in

and settled Jenny down and reversed back on to the road. Mike and Mario were waiting outside the gates of the convent. Joe stopped for them and then drove straight to the Duke where he put them in a quiet corner. They sat there, dazed and silent, while he ordered coffee.

The hot drink revived Jenny and she looked at the tired, unhappy faces of Mike and Mario. She felt herself go tense. She put down the cup unsteadily and stared into Joe's eyes. 'I must know,' she said in a small voice. 'He's dead, isn't he?'

'No,' said Joe. 'He's not dead.'

Mario suddenly crashed his fist down on the table. 'It was *our* fault!' he cried. 'It need not have happened.' Mike didn't even look up.

'Stop it!' said Joe sharply. 'It's done.'

Jenny looked from one to the other. 'What happened?'

Joe sat there and looked at her for a moment or two. She seemed fairly controlled, he thought. He rubbed his chin as he glanced at the boys. 'Simon,' he said quietly, 'is suffering from an overdose of a drug.'

'An overdose?' Jenny looked at him, her eyes startled. 'What do you mean? Pills? He got pills and ate them like sweets . . .'

'No,' said Joe flatly. 'It was heroin.'

'Heroin!' Jenny looked as if she was stunned. Then she twisted round and looked wildly at the boys. 'You don't mean . . .?'

'Yes, I do. Simon must have taken it by accident. He had some in a little silver box. It seems he got some on his fingers and sucked them—he must have taken quite a bit, but fortunately he was sick. He wouldn't have known what he was doing.'

'But what about the blood and . . .'

'He also fell. Perhaps he became dizzy. Who

knows? That's the most likely explanation.' Joe took out a cigarette and stretched his legs.

Jenny stared at him with anxious eyes. 'Was it our fault?'

'Yes, in a way it was. Mike and Mario have now said what happened this morning. If you had reported it to the police immediately they might perhaps have found Simon before he had a chance to take the heroin. As it was . . .'

'But Caldena . . .' began Jenny.

'Carlo has nothing whatever to do with it, believe me,' said Joe. 'If it hadn't been his car that was taken it would have been someone else's.'

'But what about . . .?'

Joe held up his hand and she fell silent. 'You are wrong,' he said positively. 'You are quite wrong.'

Jenny brushed her hand across her face. 'I ought to have known. I ought to have guessed.'

'I did guess,' said Mario bitterly. 'I was sure.'

'I thought it might have been,' Mike confessed.

'But you didn't say . . . you didn't hint . . .'

Mario shook his head. 'I couldn't believe it. It seemed so silly to try a landing like that in the early morning. It should have been at night—there are always people at Dwera. It seemed ridiculous.' He covered his eyes with his hands for a moment. 'How could I . . .' he murmured.

'How could I?' muttered Mike. 'Of course I had my suspicions but like you it seemed too absurd—like a bad film.'

'Was the heroin there?' asked Jenny. 'Did you find the rest of it?'

'No.' Joe picked up his cigarette from the ash-tray. 'Simon had most of the day on his own. He might have hidden it anywhere. We shall have to wait until Simon recovers . . .'

'*If* he recovers . . .' said Mario bitterly.

'*When* he recovers,' said another, deeper voice.

Jenny looked up. 'Dr Timaldi!'

Tall and thin, looking tired, he stood there, bag in one hand, the other brushing back a lock of greyish-black hair that fell over one eye. 'Cheer up,' he said. 'He won't die. He'll get better, I promise you.'

'He'll have a bad time, won't he?' said Mario.

His father nodded. 'A very bad time when he becomes conscious. It will be much worse for a child like Simon who is already unstable.' He turned to Joe. 'Will you come with me? We must report this to the police.'

'Of course,' said Joe, getting up immediately. He looked back at Jenny and Mike as he reached the door. 'Wait for me,' he said. 'I'll come back and drive you both home.'

The three of them sat there silently for a short time. Suddenly Jenny burst out. 'It's Caldena! I know it is. Did you tell them about the cigarettes, Mario?'

'No,' he said despondently, 'I didn't even think about it.'

'What's the point?' said Mike. 'He'd only deny it. They'd rather believe him than us any day.'

The three of them sat silently for a minute or two and then Jenny suddenly sat bolt upright. 'We must be blind!' she said. 'We must walk around with blinkers on!' Mike and Mario looked up. 'Who was around when Vesculdi was picked up in the Pharaoh?' she said slowly.

'Caldena!' exclaimed Mario.

'So what's significant about that?' Mike began, 'so were we and . . .' He stopped short. 'He *might* have been at the auction, I suppose,' he went on in a hesitant way.

'Oh, come off it, Mike!' snapped Jenny. 'The police were expecting an accomplice to get in touch, weren't they? And no one turned up, remember? Well, we all know why the accomplice never got there. It was because James met Caldena and told him—he actually told him, tipped him off—the idiot!' She slapped the arm of her chair. 'He had to say something, hadn't he? So what could have been better cover than the auction? There must have been hundreds of people there.'

'But why didn't he clear out when he heard Vesculdi had been nobbled?' argued Mike. 'Why hang around afterwards?'

'If he'd cleared out and there was any suspicion at all it would have looked strange, wouldn't it? He could hardly have taken off immediately James had told him. No, he did the sensible thing. He stayed put looking as if he'd every right to be there,' she declared. 'That's it. I'd bet a million I'm right.'

'You don't have to convince me,' said Mario. 'It all fits. It all adds up.'

Mike turned a determined face towards them. 'Then that settles it. I'm going with him tomorrow. I might just pick up something. You never know, he might let something slip.'

'Mike!' Jenny clutched his sleeve. 'You can't go out with him. Not after this.'

'I don't see why not,' said Mike calmly. 'Nothing's changed.'

Jenny looked at him in amazement. 'Nothing's changed?' she repeated.

'Not really. He'll know—everybody will know by now—that we found Simon but if he hasn't guessed by now that we suspect him I don't think this will make any difference.'

Mario drummed his fingers on the table. 'I think

143

it's risky, Mike. For all he knows Simon will have
told us where the heroin is.'

'No he won't. Simon isn't even conscious. He can't
have told anyone anything.'

Jenny looked up slowly and stared into Mike's eyes.
'You are right, I guess. He is, Mario, really he is.'

'I suppose so,' said Mario unhappily, 'but I still
think there is a risk.' His eyes suddenly narrowed. 'I'd
like to kill him,' he said venomously.

As Jenny placed the kaleidoscope on the table and
rolled it backwards and forwards, Mike gazed at it.
'Let's pin it on him first,' he said.

'Yes,' said Jenny, her voice hard. 'Let's do just
that.'

CHAPTER TEN

Robert dropped Mike off at Xlendi. 'Have a good day,' he said briefly, quickly reversed and drove off again without even a backward glance. Mike walked slowly along the front and over to the rocks and wandered back again. He was a bit early and there was no sign of Caldena yet. In spite of his determination to go, he had to admit to himself that he wasn't any too keen on this trip. Although the sun was blazing down there was quite a sharp warm wind. The little waves rolling down the bay were flecked with white and they slapped sharply against the wall.

A luzzu puttered in and the fisherman, with the help of a small boy, tied it up close to where Mike was standing. He glanced up. 'Not good for sailing,' he said. 'It will be rough.'

'Rough.' Mike was surprised. The sea had been nothing but serene ever since he had arrived. He couldn't imagine it any other way.

'Yes, the wind is from the south-west.' He shook his head as he stowed his gear away.

'I'm going out in a launch,' Mike said. 'That'll be all right, won't it?'

The man stared up at the sky. 'Perhaps.' He and the boy came ashore. 'Maybe it will be all right for you,' he said, 'but it is no good for me.'

Mike stared up at the sky again. The sun was so bright that he was forced to drop his eyes almost immediately. A little fleet of luzzus chugged into sight and dropped their anchors in the bay, bouncing up and down in a lively way.

'Hallo, Mike.' Caldena beamed at him as he approached. 'It's a beautiful day, isn't it?'

'I'm not so sure,' said Mike uncomfortably. 'The luzzus are coming back. As a matter of fact I was talking to a fisherman a couple of minutes ago. He said he thought it was going to blow up rough.'

'Oh!' Caldena sounded disappointed. 'Aren't you a good sailor?' he said sympathetically. 'Do you get sick easily?'

'No.' Mike's pride was stung. 'No, I'm never sick.'

'Good,' he said briskly. 'Then that is all right. Maybe it is going to blow a bit but I don't think we need worry. The luzzus don't have very big engines but James's is really powerful.' He nodded at the gleaming blue and white launch. 'I have been out to it already,' and he pointed to the little rubber dinghy that was tied up over by the rocks. Mike followed him round to it. 'You first,' Caldena said.

As Mike reluctantly put one foot in it, it danced around madly for a moment. He held on to the rock and dragged the dinghy towards him, carefully stepped in and then clung on to his handhold until Caldena was safely seated too. They each picked up a small paddle and sculled out to the launch.

It wasn't until Caldena had the engine going and they slowly picked their way out of the crowded harbour that Mike suddenly cheered up. The effect of the sun and the wind and the sheer excitement of being on a really powerful boat made him feel unexpectedly carefree.

Once they were clear and out into the open sea, Caldena opened the throttle and the boat leapt forward eagerly, her screws churning up the water behind them in a mountain of white foam. He turned to Mike. 'Round the island?' he shouted above the noise of the engine and Mike nodded back enthusiastically. He swung the wheel and the boat heeled over, righted itself and they raced on again, the wind cutting their faces like a knife so that before long their eyes were watering while their clothes were drenched with spray. Caldena cut the speed a bit. 'A good machine,' he said approvingly. 'We could go anywhere in this. Malta, Sicily, anywhere come to that.' Sicily! Mike thought. Why Sicily? What had brought that into his mind?

Caldena dropped his eyes to the instrument panel. He shook his head. 'No,' he shouted above the roar of the engine, 'not Sicily after all. There is not enough fuel. No, it is round the island, over to Comino and back again, I'm afraid, Mike.' Mike breathed a sigh of relief. The last thing he fancied was a long trip with Caldena anywhere. He watched him carefully.

As Comino loomed up, Caldena altered course so that they went round it. 'It looks deserted,' he shouted to Mike. 'But then, it is still a little early in the season.' He deftly altered course once more and they cruised into a wide turquoise blue bay where the water was so clear that the silvery bottom looked only inches away. 'The Blue Lagoon,' he said, cutting the engine so that they drifted in. 'We shall anchor here.'

Together they lowered the anchor and Caldena leaned over the side. 'It's a good place to swim,' he said. 'Let's get the ladder down.' They dragged it out and threw it over the side so that the wooden rungs clattered down into the water and the handropes were taut. Caldena stamped hard on the top rung after they had pegged it into place. 'That's all right,' he said. 'It's as firm as a rock.' He looked at Mike. 'I don't like to take risks at sea. Accidents are only too easy.'

Uneasily Mike looked around the bay. It was

empty. Only birds were moving, circling overhead and then gliding down to rest on the waves. Caldena, whistling cheerfully to himself, stripped off his thin sweater. 'Not swimming?' he asked in surprised tones, as he stood balanced on the top rung of the ladder.

'In a minute,' said Mike. 'Not just now. You go first.' His uneasiness at being alone with Caldena had returned again and although he tried to shrug it off, it was constantly in the forefront of his mind.

Caldena raised an astonished eyebrow but said nothing as he clambered down. 'Phew!' he shouted, as he splashed in. 'It is not too warm.' He struck out vigorously and swam half way towards the shore before turning back. He hooked his feet over a rung and hung on to the ladder for a moment before climbing up again. 'That was good,' he said as he picked up a towel and rubbed his face. He shook the wet hair out of his eyes as he approached Mike. 'You ought to get in.'

'No,' said Mike, 'not yet. I will soon.'

'Perhaps you should be thrown in.' Caldena's white, even teeth glinted in a thin smile.

'I'd fight back.' Mike tried hard to make it sound lighthearted.

'I think I am stronger.'

'Are you?' Mike remembered the first time he had shaken hands with Caldena. He'd been surprised even then at his strong grip. 'I'll get in in a minute,' he said, trying to sound casual.

'Yes.' Caldena turned away and flicked the towel across his back. 'I should do that.'

A flotilla of canoes swept in and circled them, the boys paddling furiously, their brown backs muscular and strong. They made for the far side of the bay and then, one by one, shouting and laughing, they plunged in. Mike felt like cheering. 'Do you know,' he said to

Caldena, 'I think I'll go in right now,' and he swung down the ladder.

Caldena was right about one thing. Apart from the initial shock, the water was marvellous. There was a buoyancy about it that he'd never experienced before. He swam around for a long time before suddenly realizing how tired he was making himself, so he sculled quietly back to the side of the launch. He hooked one foot over a rung quite high up but it was curiously slippery. He tried again and his foot slithered through the rung and became entangled in something. The boat lifted with a sudden large wave and he twisted and found himself falling backwards. The water closed over his face and, as he opened his mouth to shout, the water rushed in and partly filled his lungs. He dangled upside down and fought to right himself but the more he struggled the more his foot became enmeshed. He felt sick and faint and tried desperately to jerk himself free. It was hopeless. He felt totally waterlogged and his struggles became weaker and weaker.

As he felt himself losing consciousness a sudden friendly arm grasped him and pushed his head up while at the same time his foot worked itself free. Gasping for breath, he clung on to the lowest rung. Water poured out of his ears and nose and he shook himself feebly, coughing and spluttering at the same time, almost vomiting, his eyes streaming with water. 'All right?' said a distant voice. He nodded weakly and turned his head to see Tony's worried face looking up at him. 'Sure?' Mike nodded once more 'What happened?'

'I—I don't know. The rung was slippery—my foot was tangled. I lost my balance.'

'Lucky my team is training,' said Tony. 'It is for the muscles and the breathing.' He put a strong shoulder under Mike and lifted him higher out of the water. 'Now,' he said. 'Now try to get up. Be careful.'

Slowly and shakily Mike mounted to the deck and then dragged himself over the side. Caldena, who had been standing on the far side looking out to sea, swung round and hurried over to him, his face concerned and his eyes worried. 'Mike!' he said anxiously. 'What has happened to you?' He took hold of Mike's unresisting arm and half-carried him over to the long seat and thrust him down. 'Sit there. Don't move. I'll get you a drink.'

Tony's black head appeared above the level of the deck and then he swung his legs over and stepped on board. 'Signor Caldena,' he said. 'Mike has had a nasty surprise.'

'I know,' Caldena appeared at the entrance to the galley, a tin of coffee in his hands.

'He has nearly drowned,' Tony went on. 'Your ladder is no good.'

'No good!' Caldena paled. 'You *saw* what happened?'

'No.' Tony picked up Caldena's discarded towel and handed it to Mike. 'But before I come up I look. I see that it has extra ...' He paused for a moment, unsure how to express himself. 'Extra ropes are on the bottom like—' he twisted his fingers together to show what he meant—'like a bird's nest. There is also some grease on one rung so if you slip and you are stuck in the bird's nest, then—whoop—you are upside down. You drown.'

Caldena stood as if rooted to the spot. 'Bird's nest?' he said incredulously. 'But I've used the ladder myself.'

'I don't know. Maybe that is a rung you happened to miss. Perhaps you are just lucky. Mike was not so lucky. It was nearly the finish for a football fan. Like that it is a death trap.'

Mike stiffened and struggled up a bit. 'A death trap,' he echoed, his eyes fixed on Caldena.

Tony stood up. 'I think I must now go back.'

Anxiously Mike looked him straight in the eye. 'Don't go. Please don't go,' he urged. 'Stay and have some coffee.'

'Yes, of course.' Caldena turned to him. 'It will only take a minute.'

Tony shook his head. 'It is not good for me to drink now,' he declared. 'It is no good for training.'

'Do stay.' Mike turned his white strained face to him. 'Don't go yet.'

'Well—okay, but I will not have a drink.' He settled himself by Mike's side as Caldena arrived with two steaming mugs of coffee. He disappeared again and this time returned holding a large rug. 'Put that round yourself,' he said to Mike. 'You are still shivering.'

Gratefully Mike draped it round his shoulders while Caldena prowled restlessly round the deck. 'I do not understand,' he said. 'I just do not see how it happened.' Eventually he tapped Tony on the arm. 'Come and help me get the ladder up,' he said. 'Let us sort this out once and for all.' Together they unpegged it and hauled it out of the water. 'So that's it!' he exclaimed as they dragged it over the side. A lobster pot was entangled in the slack of the rope that dangled just beneath the water level. 'Mike! It's a wonder you didn't drown!'

'Isn't it?' said Mike drily.

Tony examined the pot carefully. 'Look,' he said, and frowned. 'It must have come away from its mooring. This is the end of the rope.'

'Someone's been fooling around with it,' said Caldena sharply. 'It looks as if it's been cut. It does not look much like an accident to me.'

'I know!' Tony slapped his thigh. 'There is great—'

he groped for the right word, 'rivalry—like between two teams, Malta and Gozo, and someone has committed a foul.'

'Rivalry?'

'Yes. Fishermen's rivalry. It could be that, maybe.' He stood and looked out to sea. 'I think it is now time for me to go. It will soon become quite rough. My team must get back to Gozo.' He gave them both a wave and then sat on the side of the boat and slipped off into the sea.

Mike felt desolate once Tony had gone. He shot a quick look at Caldena who, hands gripping his mug, was staring straight down at the deck. What was he looking so depressed for? He wasn't the one who had nearly drowned. Or was it because he, Mike, hadn't drowned? As Caldena himself had said, what could be easier than an accident at sea? A shiver started at the base of his spine and he found himself beginning to quiver all over. He pulled the rug even more tightly round himself. Don't be stupid, Mike, he said to himself. Caldena hasn't the slightest idea that we've rumbled him. Even if he had, would he be so stupid as to fix just one of them? Of course not. Whatever else Caldena was, he certainly wasn't a fool. Slowly he began to relax. He was safe enough now. One accident on one day might be explicable but two certainly wouldn't.

The sun suddenly went in and Mike glanced up to see ominous grey clouds rolling across the sky and at the same moment the launch danced up and down in a lively way as a heavy hot gust of wind blew straight into the bay. 'It's getting up,' he said.

Caldena nodded. He pointed to the white-capped waves that were rolling in towards the shore. 'One does not often see them at this time of the year,' he remarked casually.

'Hadn't we better start back?'

'Soon, maybe. But first we must eat.' He got up once again and popped down to the galley while Mike, with a slight feeling of despondency, saw Tony and his team paddling furiously in the direction of Gozo. The wind was against them and they bent low over their paddles, straining hard as they battled against the wind. 'Gosh!' he thought. 'It'll take them hours.'

Like a jack-in-the-box, Caldena reappeared, this time with two plates in his hand. Mike eyed the food hungrily. He was surprised at himself for feeling so ravenous. He took his plate eagerly while Caldena put his own down on the deck. Caldena leaned back comfortably and lit a cigarette and watched Mike. Aware of his scrutiny, Mike began to feel nervous again, and he pushed the last little bits around on his plate awkwardly.

'Mike.' Caldena stubbed out his cigarette at last and went and stood by the rails, his arms outstretched resting on them. 'There is something I must ask you.'

'Oh.' Mike kept his face as blank as possible. 'Really?'

'Yes.' Caldena took out another cigarette and lit it. He puffed quickly at it. 'I think—I do not know exactly how to put it—I think that you all think that you know something about me. I want to know what it is. I should like to clear it up. What exactly do you suspect me of?'

'Suspect? I don't *suspect* you of anything.' Mike bent over his plate so that Caldena shouldn't see his face and chased a piece of tomato around.

'Do not play games with me, Mike. I am not much of a sportsman.' The smoothness in Caldena's voice had gone. There was a rough edge to it now. 'There isn't much time.'

Mike looked up from under his lids. 'I don't know what you mean,' he said coolly. For some reason he didn't understand he felt as if he was on top of the situation.

'But you do. You know exactly what I'm talking about.' Caldena threw the cigarette away.

'Do I?'

Caldena made an effort to sound patient. 'If you would only tell me what it is you think I've done then we ...' He stopped abruptly and slammed his hand down on the railings. 'Forget me for a moment. Did Simon say anything to you?'

Mike glanced up quickly. 'Say anything? What about?'

Caldena bit his lip. 'You know perfectly well what it is I'm referring to.' Mike remained silent. A gust of wind swept his hair upright so that for a moment it looked as if he had a cock's comb. Caldena stared hard at him and then tried again. 'Please listen carefully. Everything you know about me is true. I write film-scripts. I am also a historian—not in your father's class, I grant you—and that is all there is to know.' He looked at Mike's expressionless face and clapped his hands to his head as he sat down heavily. 'How can I convince you?' he said. 'Everybody knows me. I am friendly with most people. The police have approved my application for residence ...'

'I *am* glad about that.' Mike's tone was almost insolent.

Caldena took no notice. 'What we must get our hands on is the heroin,' he said quietly.

'I bet.' Mike went pale and he clenched his fists. 'Well, you've come to the wrong person for that, haven't you? Simon found it all right, didn't he? Found, touched, took, tasted and almost died!'

'Yes, that was a tragedy.' Mike looked curiously at

Caldena. What an actor the man was! He'd even managed to make his eyes moist.

Caldena pulled out a handkerchief and unashamedly wiped them. 'It was a tragedy,' he repeated. 'Poor Simon!'

Mike's self-control snapped. He jumped to his feet, sickened by such a display of hypocrisy. 'So that's why you gave him hash, is it? That's why you encouraged him to drag. And now you sit here wiping your eyes and saying "Poor Simon". A lot you care for Simon! You must be twisted, warped inside, to do something like that. You're a pig! I'm ashamed to breathe the same air as you.' He turned away sick with rage, and leaned over the side of the boat. He just didn't care what Caldena did. It didn't matter. He closed his eyes to shut out the vision of Simon lying there, motionless, with glazed eyes and bloody leg.

'Mike!' Mike rested his head on his arms. He didn't move. 'Mike! Turn round. See what I've got!' Caldena's voice was authoritative, triumphant. Wearily Mike moved his head to look at him. There was a strange little smile on his face. 'Have a cigarette,' he said softly and very slowly drew out a plain shiny white packet. Almost unbelievingly Mike raised his eyes to Caldena and looked into his dark brown glittering ones. 'Go on, Mike,' he urged. 'Go on. Have one.'

Mike reached out his hand as if hypnotized and he slowly touched the tip. He stopped and gazed at Caldena, his mouth open.

'That's right, Mike. Help yourself. You'll like it. You'll like it as much as Simon did.'

Mike drew the cigarette out from the packet and stared at it incredulously. He lifted it to his lips and put it into his mouth and bit it. He removed the stub and stared at it once again and then he reached for the rest of the packet and tipped them all out. 'Sweets!' he said in a disbelieving voice. 'They're sweets! I haven't seen them since I was a kid.'

'Nor me. I have them made for Simon. It gives him much pleasure.' Caldena tossed the empty packet to Mike. 'Examine it, Mike. You will see it is identical to the one Jenny found.

'You knew about it?' Mike was astounded.

'Of course.' Caldena got up and stared across the bay at the rising waves. 'Perhaps I should have guessed what you thought it contained. If I had we could have cleared all this up sooner and maybe Simon . . .'

'I know.' Mike felt guilty even just thinking of him. 'I hope they get them for it. I hope they put them away for a good long stretch.'

Caldena went into the cabin and switched on the engine. 'You are quite sure, Mike, that you have no idea whatsoever where the heroin is? You see, they'll be totally unscrupulous. They are dangerous men. That shipment is worth a great deal of money.'

Mike shook his head. 'Honestly,' he said, 'we haven't got a clue. Only Simon knows and you know him, he might not even remember and even if he does he might not tell.' He looked curiously at Caldena. 'Have you any idea who they are? Are they local?'

'No.' Caldena opened the throttle as the engine roared into life. They could be anyone. The island's full of visitors right now. However, the police are not sleeping, I can tell you that. You are, I hope, satisfied now that I am not part of the gang?'

'Sure.' Mike grinned at him. 'It's a pity in a way. You fitted the bill so well.' They roared out of the bay and stood side by side watching Mgarr grow larger and larger until Caldena swung the boat round in a wide arc and they made for Xlendi. He nodded across to the far side as they tied up. 'There are your friends,' he said, 'looking very relieved to see you safely back. Even if I had been a—big wheel in the Mafia—I really don't think I would have dared to come back without you. You're lucky to have friends like that.' He put a restraining hand on Mike's arm just before he got into the little rubber dinghy. 'Wait a minute. There is just one more thing.' He hurried to the cabin and came up with a large sealed brown envelope. 'This is for you all.'

Mike ripped it open and fumbled inside. His groping fingers touched a sheet of thickish paper. 'Be careful,' said Caldena.

As Mike tipped up the envelope a sheet fell out of it on to the seat. He glanced at it quickly and then peered closely. Open-mouthed he looked up into Caldena's delighted face and then he gazed down at the paper once more. He put his finger to one edge and ran it down it. 'The other half of the map!' he cried, his face beaming with pleasure. 'Where did it come from? How did you get hold of it? How did you know?'

'It's from Malta, from an antiquarian bookshop. When I first caught that glimpse of it in Jenny's hands in the Pharaoh it rang a bell. It immediately reminded me of something—something I'd seen recently—so I went and had a word with Mr Alberghini and when he told me that what Jenny had was only half of a chart, I felt certain that I'd seen the other half somewhere. I simply couldn't remember at first and then suddenly—in the middle of Mr Albion's party, to be exact—I knew where I'd seen it. I was so positive that I went straight across and bought it.' His round face broke into a happy smile.

'Incredible! Fantastic!' exclaimed Mike. 'It'll bowl Jenny over, I can tell you that.'

Caldena gave him a friendly pat on the shoulder. 'Good,' he said. 'I hoped it would be a success, but I think that you'd better go and reassure your friends. They look impatient. They probably can't imagine why I seem to be detaining you.'

Mike carefully returned the map to the envelope. 'It'll be a fantastic surprise,' he said.

'But not quite the surprise Jenny was expecting,' said Caldena, as he held the dinghy fast for Mike to climb in.

As Mike sculled himself ashore and walked across to the others, Jenny ran up to him, her face a mixture of relief and pleasure. 'Oh, Mike!' she cried, throwing her arms around him. 'Thank goodness you're back. We should never have let you go out with him. I've been having nightmares about it. I couldn't guess what Caldena might do—but I knew he'd stop at nothing if he had the slightest idea you knew and you're such a rotten actor, you said so yourself.' She gripped his arm tightly as though she'd never let go.

Mario strolled up to him more casually, his hands in his pockets. 'There you are,' he said to Jenny. 'I told you he'd be all right, didn't I?' Then he suddenly smiled broadly at Mike and thumped him on the back. 'It was okay, wasn't it? No trouble? It was all right?'

'Sure.' Mike looked at them both with a straight face. He put his hand into his pocket and slowly drew out a familiar shiny white packet and held it out. 'Have a cigarette,' he said.

CHAPTER ELEVEN

Jenny pulled the bell. It clanged loudly and then died down to a faint tinkle and finally stopped. The door was opened by a quiet-faced nun who looked enquiringly at her. 'May I see Simon?' she asked, twiddling nervously with the strap of her bag.

The nun stood there for a moment or two before she said, 'I will go and speak to Mother Superior. Please come this way.' She led the way up an almost antiseptically clean passage and opened the door of a cool, sparsely-furnished room. 'Please wait here,' she said.

Jenny went straight to the window and stood looking out at the tiny little cloister where two nuns, their hands clasped in front of them and their eyes downcast, walked serenely round and round.

'Yes?' Surprised, Jenny swung round. She hadn't heard anyone come into the room. Mother Superior, surprisingly young and calm-faced, looked directly at her with friendly eyes.

'I just wondered,' said Jenny, 'if I might visit Simon?'

'Are you a relative?'

'No.' Jenny shook her head so hard that her long fair hair swung heavily round her shoulders. 'No. I'm not . . .'

Mother Superior shook her head in her turn. 'Then I am sorry,' she said. 'I am afraid that Simon has been seriously ill. He has suffered a great deal. Too many visitors . . .'

'I know,' said Jenny quickly. 'At least, I can guess. Please let me see him. Honestly, I'm one of Simon's oldest friends. I was one of the ones who found him. I mean, if he's well enough to see anyone I know he'd like to see me. Really he would. Look,' she fished in her bag and brought out the kaleidoscope. 'I've brought this for him. It's his favourite thing. He calls it klally.'

Mother Superior smiled at last. She put her cool hand on Jenny's. 'So this is klally,' she said. 'He's been asking for it. We none of us could imagine what it was. Come along.'

She continued down the long bare corridor, led the way up a short flight of stairs and halted outside a door. 'You do understand what happened to Simon, don't you? He actually ate some heroin. Luckily he brought most of it up, otherwise he would have died. Most of the time since he came out of his coma he has been quiet, but occasionally he becomes very disturbed. Don't worry. We all know what to do. Just try not to excite him too much. I shall wait out here for you. If you find he does not want to talk to you then just come away. You can try again another time.'

She opened the door and ushered Jenny into a gay little room with bright curtains at the window and a brilliant rug on the highly polished floor. 'Simon,' she said, 'you're a lucky boy today. I've brought you another visitor.' She smiled encouragingly at Jenny and slipped outside again.

Simon continued to lay there, his face expressionless, gazing vacantly at the ceiling. He didn't even move his head as Jenny approached. She moved forward a pace or two. 'Simon,' she said. 'It's me. It's Jenny.' There wasn't even a flicker of an eyelid. Jenny moved a little closer. 'Simon,' she said again. 'I've come to see you.' She knocked the leg of the chair and he flinched. 'Look,' she said, 'I'm going to sit down and talk to you.'

She settled down and sat quietly for a few moments. Simon's head rolled a little to one side and she caught a glimpse of his dull eyes. 'I've got a present for you,' she said. His head rolled over a little more. 'It's not a new present,' she went on, 'it's an old one, but I know you'll like it.' His mouth twitched slightly. Feeling encouraged Jenny said, 'If you put out your hand I'll give it to you.'

Simon's arm shot out unexpectedly quickly. Jenny gasped. Although it was mainly covered by a plaster she could see that there was a long deep gash up it and it was still swollen and badly bruised. She said nothing however but put the kaleidoscope into his palm.

He gripped it tightly and then pulled it under the thin cover. 'Klally,' he murmured, 'klally.' His mouth grew wet and his eyes brightened a little. She could see him caressing it under the sheet. 'Klally.'

Jenny moved a little closer. 'Do you want me to bring you anything else?' she asked.

He turned one bloodshot eye to her and for the first time she saw the deep grazes on his face. 'Choc,' he mumbled. 'Choc.'

'I'll bring it next time, Simon,' she promised. 'Come on, Simon, sit up and talk to me. I've come especially to see you.'

He shifted a little and Jenny helped him to move and propped his pillows up a bit. She could now see that on the other side of his head part of his hair had been cut away and there was another plaster. The bruises and swellings spread from his forehead to his chin. 'Oh, Simon!' she cried.

He thumped the kaleidoscope from one palm to the other. 'Klally, klally.' He tried to smile but a spasm of pain crossed his face. 'Hurts!' he shouted and put his hand to his face.

Jenny glanced anxiously at the closed door. 'Sh!' she said. She didn't want to be turned out yet. 'Simon, what happened to your packet? Where did you put it?'

His eyes rolled around and he stared vacantly at the ceiling once more. The corners of his mouth turned down and his chin wobbled. Tears formed in his eyes and began to drip silently down his face. 'Don't cry, Simon,' she said hastily, grabbing a tissue and wiping them away. 'It'll be all right. I'll bring a big bar of chocolate soon.'

His head moved a little closer to her. 'Big choc?' he whispered.

'Yes,' she said earnestly. 'Very big. The biggest one I can find. Now, Simon, try to think. You picked up the packet from the water, didn't you?' He nodded his head up and down. 'What happened after that.'

He thrust his arm out again. 'Fell down,' he mumbled. 'Simon fell.'

'Poor arm.' Jenny tucked it in again. 'Then what did you do?'

He fell silent again and rolled his head over so that he could look out of the window. He ran his tongue over his lips. 'In the box,' he said.

'That's right,' said Jenny. 'You put some in the box. That was for you. What did you do with the rest?'

'Silver,' he said.

'Yes, I know. It was a silver box.'

Simon tried to shake his head. 'Silver,' he said again. He caught hold of Jenny's arm and tried to pull her towards him. 'Mine,' he whispered. 'Simon's.'

'Of course it is,' she said hastily, seeing the tears collecting again in the corners of his eyes.

He regarded her doubtfully for a moment. 'Silver,' he said. 'The lady.'

162

'What lady?' Jenny bent over him.

He brought out the kaleidoscope and banged it in his palm again. 'Lady!' he roared. He opened his mouth and screamed. 'Hurts!' He scratched at his plaster. 'Hurts. Simon hurts! Ow—ow—oh!' He began to shriek over and over again and banged his arm against the wall.

The door opened quickly and Mother Superior and another nun came in together. As Mother Superior took Jenny by the arm and led her away, the other nun picked up a glass of pink liquid and held it to his mouth. Simon began to scream louder and louder, as if he was an animal caught in a trap and the screams followed Jenny and Mother Superior all the way down the stairs. It wasn't until they were in the waiting-room and the door was tightly shut that they were cut off. Mother Superior shot a quick look at Jenny and led her to a chair. 'Just sit down for a moment,' she said.

Obediently Jenny sat down, her face white. 'That was horrible.' she said. 'Does it happen all the time?'

'No,' said Mother Superior briskly. 'You were unfortunate.'

'Will he get better?' asked Jenny.

'Oh, yes. He's well on the road to recovery now. The bruises and cuts will clear up, of course. He did those himself. For the rest—well, it will take time but Simon has great resilience. Dr Timaldi said that practically any other child would surely have died. We must thank God for giving Simon such a strong constitution.'

'Thank God!' said Jenny bitterly. 'What for? If he hadn't been born like he was it wouldn't have happened at all. He . . .' Her eyes suddenly flooded with tears and she hastily pulled out her handkerchief and blew her nose. 'Sorry,' she said. 'I didn't mean to do that. I just hadn't thought what sort of state Simon would be in. Poor kid. It'll be something he'll never forget.'

Mother Superior led the way to the front door. 'I think you are wrong,' she said quietly as she opened it. 'Simon has suffered and will suffer again but I am sure that he will be able to shut this memory away in a corner of his mind. He will be happy in time!'

'I hope you're right,' said Jenny grimly. 'But I can tell you this. It's not a memory I'd want to have in my mind, shut away or not.' She turned back. 'Thank you,' she said. 'I'm sorry if I have behaved badly. Can I come again?'

Mother Superior smiled at her. 'I shall be delighted if you do,' she said.

As Jenny walked down the path and out of the gates, Nick got out of the car and came towards her. 'Good God!' he exclaimed. 'You look as if you've had a nasty shock, Jenny.

'Yes.' Jenny got in and sat down. She leaned forward thoughtfully. 'Mother Superior says he's much better. Heaven knows what he was like before. He began screaming while I was there and knocking his arm about.'

'Could the poor devil be suffering from withdrawal symptoms?' asked Al. 'I mean, he did swallow some of the stuff, didn't he?'

'It was only the tiniest bit,' said Jenny. 'If he'd swallowed what he shoved in his mouth he'd have kicked the bucket. There's no doubt about that.'

Al punched the wheel of the car viciously. 'It makes you want to throw up, doesn't it?' he said. 'The things people do for money. It's murder!'

'Calm down,' said Nick. 'Once is bad enough but at least he'll never be able to lay his hands on any more.'

'Won't he though?' said Al. 'After all, no one's found the stuff he's hidden, have they, Jenny?'

'No.' She shook her head. 'I'd like to know where it is myself.'

'So would we,' said Nick. 'So would everybody else on the island. It's dangerous.'

'I did try to get it out of him,' Jenny said, 'but I didn't get very far.'

'I didn't realize,' Nick said, 'that he could actually speak that clearly.'

'Oh, yes.' Jenny sat back again. 'He doesn't know many words and it's not easy to understand, but he can manage.'

Al switched the ignition on. 'Where do you want to go?' he asked. 'The place is pretty busy this morning. It's getting like Piccadilly Circus in Victoria right now.'

'Busy?' Jenny wrinkled her forehead.

'The festa, Jenny! It's the festa. You can't have forgotten about it.'

'Do you know, Al, I had? All I thought about this morning was seeing Simon. It's a pity he's going to miss it. Did you know he's taken a silver box from the church? He thinks it's his now. He just kept on about that and a lady. I can't imagine what he meant. Nothing I suppose.'

Al slammed the car into gear and they moved off. 'Where to?' he asked.

'Drop me at the crossroads,' she said. 'I want to tell Mario about Simon.'

Al stopped again. 'Then we're going the wrong way,' he said. 'Mario's having a look round those buildings, the ones where you found Simon. I think he feels that there might be some sort of a clue to the hiding place there.'

'So he is,' said Nick. 'Shall we drive you there, Jenny?'

'No thanks. I'll walk. It isn't far.'

'Certain? We're going to go in that direction anyway,' said Al. 'We're off to have a look at a place near Gharb.' He reversed the car. 'It seems silly to leave you to walk.'

'It won't do me any harm for once,' she said, and strode off.

Nick looked at Al as they overtook her. 'She's a nice kid,' he said. 'I don't like leaving her like this.'

Al watched her in the mirror. 'Neither do I,' he said thoughtfully.

Mike sat in Arthur's café, a half-cold cup of tea in front of him, and watched as the decorations for the festa were put up. Everything, it seemed, that was even vaguely possible, was thrown in to create a suitable air of festivity. Garlands, paper chains, coloured lights, wreaths over wooden figures standing on podiums, set pieces for fireworks, old Christmas decorations, flowers, flags: all were draped, twisted, entwined and hung from every possible place. Mike wouldn't have been a bit surprised if the proverbial kitchen sink had been hoisted up a lamp-post.

'Good, huh?' Arthur, his face beaming, plonked himself down by Mike. 'Very good display. The best in the island.'

'Fabulous!' Mike gazed out into the street. It was packed with people—people shopping and watching, drinking and talking. 'When does it all start?'

Arthur shrugged. 'Eight,' he said. 'Nine, maybe.' He smiled broadly. 'What does it matter?'

'You haven't seen Mario this morning?'

'No.' Arthur got to his feet. 'Wait.' He went out into the street and brought back Freddie, who was holding a large bunch of flowers in one hand and a hammer in the other. He tried to shake Mike's hand with the hammer and Mike jerked its head up and down politely. 'Good morning,' he said.

'I just wondered if you'd seen Mario?'

Freddie clutched at the slipping flowers. 'Mario? Yes, I saw him with the dark Englishman this morning.'

'Nick,' said Mike.

'Al,' said Arthur.

'Yes,' said Freddie and hurried out.

'There you are,' said Arthur proudly. 'Now you know.'

'What do we know?' asked Mike.

'That he was with Al.'

'Nick.'

'No, only with Al.'

Arthur turned as someone else came in. 'Ah! Mrs Sue.' He hastily wiped Mike's table down and pulled out a chair for her. 'Coffee,' he said decisively. 'You need coffee.'

Sue dumped her heavy shopping basket on the floor. 'I need something,' she said. 'It's hard work today. How are you, Mike?'

'Fine.' He moved his legs around restlessly under the table and then took a deep breath. 'Sue,' he said, his face serious, 'Jenny and Mario and I have made absolute fools of ourselves and . . .'

'I know,' she said calmly. 'Poor old Carlo. Still, he's got a sense of humour, luckily. He won't hold it against you.'

Mike stared at her in amazement. 'Sue!' he exclaimed. 'What *don't* you know!'

Sue smiled at him. 'Quite a lot,' she said. 'I'm not exactly in the Inspector's confidence, you know, but you don't have to be a genius to put two and two together. You're a rotten sleuth, Mike. You've been barking up the wrong tree all the time.'

'I know,' he said dejectedly. 'If my father knew he'd be furious.'

'He won't,' she said with certainty. 'No one will tell him, I promise you.' She looked round. 'Where's Jenny?'

'I was looking for her and Mario. I thought we all ought to apologize properly to Mr Caldena.'

'I should.' She turned to Arthur who had brought her coffee. 'Thanks,' she said. She turned back to Mike. 'I don't think you lot should do any more private eyeing. I have a feeling that things are going to hot up round here. You want to keep out of it.'

'Oh!' He looked at her, his face interested. 'What for instance?'

'It's just a feeling.' Sue concentrated on stirring her coffee. 'What I mean is, you just leave everything to the police from now on. They know exactly what they are doing.' She glanced out. 'Look, there's Mario. He's crossing the square.'

He jumped up. 'Do you mind?' he asked, and galloped across. But he was too late. By the time he'd dodged in and out of the traffic Mario was out of sight again. He walked down the road rather aimlessly, kicking a small stone in front of him until it fell into the gutter, and then he stopped at the crossroads and stood, uncertain of what to do next.

James, coming up the hill in his Land-Rover, spotted Mike standing there and he squealed to a halt. 'Let's get out of this,' he shouted. 'Place is full of foreigners. Come and have a swim.'

Pleased at almost any suggestion, Mike climbed in beside him and clutched the seat as James rocketed down the road. 'Is Jenny there?' he asked.

'No.' James swung the Land-Rover round a sharp corner. 'Went out early. Said something about Simon. She'll probably spend most of the day with him.' They lurched over the bridge and zoomed down the hill to Xlendi. 'Wearing your swimming trunks?' he asked. 'All right. I'll go and change. I'll meet you on the rocks.'

Mike had a quick swim before James came back and he sat on the warm seat, his arms round his knees, and looked about. High on the cliffs on either side, almost completely hidden by the old fort on one side and by the bulge of the cliff-face on the other, he could see khaki-clad men busily snaking a cable along the edge of the cliffs. They seemed totally unconcerned by the precariousness of their position as they swung out on ropes.

By the time James came down, they were gone. 'There were some soldiers up on the top,' Mike said to him. 'I wonder what they were doing?'

James scanned the cliffs. 'No sign of them now,' he grunted. 'Waste of time, I expect. They have to keep them busy. It's the same everywhere.'

'What do you think the cable's for?'

'Cable?' James scanned the cliffs once again. 'I can't see any cable. Are you sure?'

Lazily Mike lifted his eyes. There was nothing to be seen. 'I guess you're right,' he said. 'It must have been an exercise or something.'

James peeled off his robe and patted his swelling stomach. 'Coming in?' he asked, and plunged in with a great splash. He shook his head when he came out again so that Mike was splattered with great drops of sea-water. 'Just going out to the launch,' he said, 'to see she's all right. Better get her filled up this afternoon.'

Mike stood up as well. 'Do you need any help?' he asked. He didn't particularly feel like working on the boat but he knew how much pleasure it gave James to have someone to show off to.

169

'No. Don't think so,' said James. 'Just want to satisfy myself that Caldena didn't mess her about. Tell you what, Mike, you go down to St Patrick's and order lunch for us. I'll come and join you there.'

'All right.' Mike stretched himself out again in the sun and shut his eyes. 'I'll go in a few minutes.'

'Better go now,' said James. 'They might be busy later. Don't want to go without, do we?'

Mike was mildly surprised. They never had had to go without but he scrambled up and wandered there. Once there, of course, he found it too much trouble to go back and so he sat in a doze while James went out to the boat. It was the roar of the engines that surprised him. James was zooming out of the bay. 'Well,' he said to himself, 'he might have taken me with him.'

However, James was soon back. 'Filled her up,' he said. 'Don't like to run short.'

After lunch Mike began to feel restless again. 'Jenny's been a long time, hasn't she?' he remarked.

James looked up from his book. 'Longer the better,' he said. 'She's always buzzing around like a fly. More peaceful here without her.'

Mike tried to settle down to read too but he found that he simply couldn't concentrate. At last he saw Mario's van bumping round the corner and he jumped to his feet and waved. 'So long, James,' he said. 'See you at the festa, I guess.'

'Not on your life,' James grunted, lifting his eyes for a moment. 'All that pushing and shoving up there. Not my idea of fun.'

Mike and Mario met half-way along the front. 'Seen Jenny?' they said to each other.

'James said she went to see Simon,' said Mike, 'but that was this morning. She hasn't been back yet. Maybe they're letting her stay with him for a bit.'

Mario pursed his lips. 'It's not very likely,' he said, after a pause. 'My father says that Simon's still weak. If she sees him at all it'll only be for a few minutes.'

'Then where do you think she is?'

'Knocking round Victoria, probably,' said Mario. 'We must just keep missing each other.' He hesitated for a moment. 'Why don't we go and leave messages everywhere? Someone's sure to bump into her sooner or later.'

Half-way up the hill they met Al's blue Triumph coming down and they both stopped. Al's sandy head poked out of the window. 'Hi!' he said enthusiastically. 'Long time no see.'

'You haven't seen Jenny, have you?'

'Yep. Saw, spoke, smelled and touched. She was all there.'

'When was that?'

'Not sure. Twelveish, I should think. Why?'

'Can't find her, that's all.'

'But she's looking for you,' said Nick, leaning over to talk to them. 'You must be playing hide and seek.'

'Where was she?'

'Near the Xaghra crossroads. We'd given her a lift to the convent. She said she was going to look for you.'

'Ha!' said Al. 'I see it all. She has been swept away by a tall, dark stranger, entranced by her beauty and charm, and is, e'en now, incarcerated in some dark and vile dungeon, waiting for a white knight in shining armour to rescue her.'

'A likely story,' sneered Nick. 'No, I should think she's pattering around Victoria. You'll probably run into her.'

'I hope so,' said Mike. 'It's getting on.'

Nick looked at his watch, 'So it is,' he said. 'It's nearly five. Come on, Al. Let's get back and spruce ourselves up for the jamboree.'

'I'll tell you what,' said Mario, as they crawled up the hill. 'I'll drop you at your house and I'll go back to Victoria and leave a message in the Duke and another one with Arthur and we'll all meet on the steps of the church at about eight thirty.'

'Fine,' Mike said. He looked at Mario. 'You do think she's all right, don't you?'

'She can't have come to any harm,' said Mario. 'Not on Gozo.'

Bruised and battered, Jenny lay on the earth floor in a semi-conscious state for some time. At last she groaned and began to move. Every movement brought a fresh spasm of pain, but she slowly levered herself up and leaned against the rough wall. Her face felt odd and she put her fingers up to it and then gazed stupidly at them. They were sticky with blood. Gingerly she felt again. She'd got a small cut over her left eye that felt fairly deep. It wasn't actually running with blood, though. It felt tacky, as if it was forming into a scab.

She rested her head in her hands and tried to think. Where was she? That was the first thing. It was gloomy in the room. It smelt musty too. It wasn't too dark to see the little door in the far corner and so, swaying a little, she got to her feet and stumbled on rubbery legs across to it. She gave it a hard push and it opened so easily that she almost fell out. She poked her head round cautiously. There didn't seem to be anyone about. The place was silent. She stepped outside and stood in the covered passageway. Behind her was a flight of steps that clearly led to an open terrace and in front of her was a solid door—the front door, she supposed. She moved to it and grabbed the handle and pushed hard. Wrong way, she thought to herself, and gave it a hard tug instead. It was no good. It didn't give an inch. Furiously, careless of any noise she might make, she banged and kicked at it and then banged again, yelling at the top of her voice at the same time. She stopped and listened. There wasn't a sound. It was deserted.

She went back to the stairs and sat down and tried to put her confused thoughts into some sort of order. What on earth had happened? She put one hand up to her aching head and felt a large bump beneath her hair. She fingered it meditatively. Suddenly something clicked into place. Those old buildings! That was it. That was where she'd been clobbered. Mario hadn't been there. She remembered that. She'd called his name then—whonk! She ran her fingers carefully over the swelling. So, if Mario hadn't been there, then who had? She suddenly took a deep breath. Al and Nick! That who it was! It was them. It simply had to be. Who else knew she was going there? Come to that, who had *told* her to go there? Why? What for? The whole thing seemed mad.

Suddenly she crashed her fist into her palm. Simon! Now she'd got it. He'd told her where the heroin was and she hadn't been smart enough to put two and two together straight away. The silver lady! 'Silver' and 'lady', that's what he'd said. It was in the statue of Our Lady. She groaned aloud at her own stupidity. It had taken her long enough to get there. Nick and Al must have cottoned on immediately. They'd quietly put her out of the way until they'd got the stuff safely away.

Angrily she paced up and down the passage. She was furious with herself. It must have been like snatching candy from a baby to them. She rushed back to the door and kicked it viciously and shouted and yelled again. It was no good. It was as silent as the grave.

173

Well, she thought, they weren't getting away with it. She flung round and hurtled up the steps to the terrace, open to the sky. It was totally enclosed. Anxiously she looked up. It was already getting dark. She pushed open one of the three doors that opened on to it and hurried across the empty room to the window. It was boarded up but she put her eye to a chink and squinted out. She could see nothing but the blank wall of another building nearby. She raced into the next room and the next. It was hopeless.

She went back on to the terrace and eyed the little tower tucked in one corner and kicked at its door until it swung open, only to reveal a narrow twisting flight of stairs. She ran up them eagerly and then stopped at the top, her face white. She was on a narrow balcony surrounding the square courtyard below. She caught her breath and leaned back against the wall, nervously holding on to the door post with both hands. Cautiously, not risking a downward glance, she stared along the narrow little walk. The wooden balustrade surrounding it was rotten and broken but on the far side was yet another room. If only she could get there she might be able to make someone hear. She knew it was her only hope.

Suddenly the resolution in her face faded. She put her hands to her face. She had a feeling of utter despair. She couldn't get out and she couldn't—she knew she couldn't—walk round that narrow rotting balcony. She was trapped by her own fear of heights, of falling, of toppling through the frail wood, of landing with a sickening thud on those hard cold tiles underneath. Her legs felt weak. They weren't going to hold her up much longer. Carefully she slipped to the ground and sat there, her head in her hands, completely helpless.

CHAPTER TWELVE

Mike and Mario sat together in Arthur's café. Arthur himself, resplendent in black suit and pink striped shirt, an extravagant tie and a bowler hat, his heavy gold watch chain stretched across a fawn waistcoat, stood proudly at the counter, his wrinkled face glowing with happiness. 'Pretty good, huh?' he said, waving a proprietorial arm around the café.

Mario and Mike, their heads nearly brushing a dangling paper chain, looked round too at the little string of coloured lights; at the little plaster saint, fresh flowers and a candle at her feet; at the draped flags of Malta and Britain and the pennant below that said 'Isle of Wight'. They grinned back.

'Pretty good,' Mike said, in an impressed tone.

Outside, as it became darker, the crowds grew thicker. Jostling, shoving, laughing, talking, the Gozitans were getting ready for their festa. Mike felt that he could almost put out a hand and touch the excitement that was building up.

Mario nudged him. 'It's getting on,' he said. 'Funny Jenny's not turned up yet.'

'Oh, I don't know,' Mike said carelessly. 'She's probably doing herself up. You know what girls are.'

'We could go and pick her up. She won't get a lift from James, that's for sure. He won't leave Xlendi while this is going on.'

'Okay.' Mike was pleased at the idea of action. 'Let's do that.'

They left Arthur and started threading their way

through the people who spilled over from one side of the road to the other. It was almost completely dark and the faint glimmering of the fairy lights in the trees grew stronger and stronger minute by minute. Every corner had a saint safely tucked away in a little box, with flickering candles and flowers round him. While every balcony, draped with flags, paper chains, banners or just rich glowing cloths, was packed with people, while the scent of flowers permeated the air. One after another fantastic illuminations sprang into life, and people, their faces happy and flushed, all dressed in their best, expanded into every square inch of space.

Mario's excited face turned round. 'Come on. This way,' he shouted, seeing Mike's reddish hair just above the crowd. 'Push!' At last, panting and dishevelled, they broke through the crowd and emerged on the far side of the crossroads. 'There she is,' Mario said, pointing to his van. He looked back up the road. 'We shan't be able to get as close as this when we come back though. We'll have to park miles away. Still, at least Jenny won't have to slog up the hill.'

Nick and Al emerged from the Duke and waved. 'We're just off to get Jenny,' Mike called to them. 'Do you want anything from Xlendi?'

'Too late, dear boy, too late,' Nick shouted back.

'That's right,' crowed Al, 'we've already laid our grubby hands on her. She's ours for the night, not yours.' They sauntered towards the boys.

Mike looked round. 'Where is she? Is she still in the Duke?' He started off towards it.

'No, no, no.' Al put out a hand to stop him. 'She's steamed off to have a last word with Simon before the festivities begin.'

'She thought he might be a bit upset by the noise and all that,' Nick added. 'We're meeting her later.'

'Of course. We should have thought of that for ourselves.' Mario turned a disgusted face to Mike. 'I shouldn't think she'll be all that long, though. My father said only this evening that Simon still needed lots of rest. I should think Mother Superior will chuck her out pretty quickly.'

'We could pick her up from there,' said Mike. 'We can hardly miss her.'

'Only too easily I should think,' said Nick. 'Look at the cars pouring in. She's probably got a lift anyway.'

'Where are you meeting her?' asked Mike.

'My dear fellow,' Al said, 'you don't think we're telling you that. We've got her and we're keeping her. She's all ours for the evening, lucky girl.' Someone weaved past him, a happy grin on his face and a bottle in his hand. He took off the paper hat he was wearing and stuck it on Al's head. Al fingered it. A delighted smile spread across his face. 'A crown, no less. Well, well, what could be more suitable?'

A gang of girls, dazzlingly attired, their hair shining, arms linked together, came half-skipping, half-dancing up the road. One of them seized Nick's arm and he was borne off with them, laughing and shouting as he went. 'Lucky devil,' said Al. 'Never mind. There are compensations. The fair Jenny's all mine.'

Mike found himself surrounded by some boys and then he too was swept away from the others for a moment. By the time he'd fought his way back to Mario, he was alone. 'Where's Al?' he asked.

Mario shrugged. 'I turned round to see what had happened to you and when I looked back he'd gone. Now we still don't know where they are meeting Jenny.'

'We're bound to bump into her sooner or later.'

Mario looked at the swelling crowds doubtfully. 'I suppose so,' he said. 'The best thing we can do is to

make for the square. We can stand on the steps and
see everything that's going on and keep an eye open
for her at the same time.' They started off again,
weaving their way in and out of the crowds.

It was the sudden loud chiming of a great bell
almost in her ears that made Jenny look up again.
The reverberations almost made the house shudder as
it tolled over and over again. She shook herself. What
was that? Eight or nine? The sky was now a misty
bluish-purple. Nine, she decided. Once again the
hopelessness of her position struck her. What could she
do? There was no point in going down—nobody
seemed to be about—and she couldn't possibly go up.
As she stared across the open well again, she looked
once more at the open door on the far side. There was
a brighter patch of light in that room. It was another
window but unlike the others, it wasn't boarded up. If
only she could get there, maybe she'd be able to get
some help.

With sudden resolution, her eyes fixed firmly on the
end wall, she began to crawl towards it. 'Just don't
look down, Jenny,' she muttered to herself, 'just don't
look down. It's safe. You'll be all right.' She
negotiated the first corner safely and started on the
next leg of her journey. It was when she was almost
within reach of the door that her foot slipped and she
felt it hanging unsupported over the edge. Panic
began to rise and she gave herself a mental shake.
'Drag it in, you fool. That's better.'

Even when she reached the door she simply couldn't
bring herself to stand on the balcony at all so she
crawled into the little room and only then stood up.
She rushed to the window and thrust it open eagerly.
There, far below, looking like tiny specks, were
people, hundreds of people. Curiously unafraid now

that she had something to hang on to, she leaned out. 'Help!' she shouted. 'Help! Help!' Not one head looked up. She made a trumpet of her hands and tried again, screaming at the top of her voice until she was hoarse. Still not a head moved in her direction. She could just hear the distant thumping of a band. Of course no one could hear her with that sort of row going on. There wasn't a hope in hell. She stood by the door for a moment. Well, at least it had told her something, that and the great bell. She was in the Citadel, locked away in one of those empty houses probably.

The sky suddenly exploded with noise all around her as petard after petard was set off and showers of fireworks whooshed up into the air, exploded and hung there motionless, suspended in blackness before drifting down in a fountain of sparks. Bursts of music, laughter and cheering drifted faintly up to her ears and she bit her lip furiously. Suddenly she heard pattering coming from the other side of the house, the cathedral side. It was someone running, someone who was still some distance away, but someone who was coming towards her. She looked at the balcony once again and sucked in her breath. This was no time for crawling. If she did that she'd be too late. She'd have to get round a bit quicker this time.

Her face set, her arms and shoulders pressed firmly against the wall, she edged her way round as fast as she dared. The one thing above all that she dared not risk was stopping. So, lips pressed tightly together, she inched her way along, her head well up, and at last thankfully touched the end wall. There was one short stride to take after that and then she touched the last obstacle, the roof. Spurred by the nearness of the footsteps she forced herself to scramble up and then made directly for the low parapet. Her face paled as she looked down. She was high above the narrow passage separating the cathedral from the row of houses. She gripped the edge tightly and stared anxiously at the end of the passage where it met the cathedral square.

Tony, in running shorts and vest, his arms swinging high, trotted round the corner. Jenny almost laughed. Who but Tony would rather miss the festa than a training session? 'Tony!' she shouted. 'Tony!'

He was so surprised he almost stopped jogging. He rotated, still running up and down on the spot, and looked up and down the passage.

'Tony! I'm up here! On the roof!'

He jerked his head up. 'Hallo,' he said and started off again.

'Tony! Help me! I can't get out!'

'Sure,' he shouted amiably, 'when I've finished my training.'

Recklessly Jenny leaned over even further. 'Please!' she cried desperately. 'Please, you've got to help me *now*!'

Tony did a few little steps backwards. 'I have nearly finished,' he called back. 'I will not be long.'

Jenny beat at the wall in her fury. 'Tony! Get that door open somehow. Bash it in. Kick it down. I don't care what you do, but *do* something.'

He stopped prancing up and down and looked up at her in amazement. 'Now,' he said reproachfully, 'I will have to start it all over again. You have spoiled it.'

'Get it open!' she screamed. 'Get an axe. Break it down.'

Tony looked up at her once more. 'You want me to break it open?' he asked doubtfully.

Jenny clapped her hands to her head in despair. 'I've got to get out. I don't care how you do it. Just get me out.'

'Okay,' he said. 'I'll turn the key.' He shook his head as he went towards the door. 'It is bad to leave the key in the door like that,' he said reprovingly. 'It is a temptation.'

Reaction had set in for Jenny. Now she just couldn't make it across that roof again and drop down on to that balcony. She couldn't risk slipping and falling against the rotting balustrade. Her legs began to shake and she felt sick. She grasped the parapet once more. 'Tony,' she said. 'I can't get down, Tony. Please come and help me.'

'Sure,' he said. 'I will run.' She heard him pounding up the stairs and within seconds his head appeared at the door of the little turret. 'I'm here,' he said proudly. 'That was pretty quick, huh?'

Jenny stretched out a shaking hand to him. 'I can't walk along that balcony again,' she said faintly. 'I don't think I can even get off the roof.'

'Sure you can.' Tony ran surefootedly along the balcony and vaulted on to the roof. He strode across to her. 'Look, you hold me. I'll take you down.'

'Oh, Tony!' Jenny couldn't understand why she was crying, and neither could she stop the tears that rolled down her face. She tried to smile through them. 'Tony!' she said again. He put one arm round her shoulders and held her hand tightly.

'Listen,' he said, 'we shall go slowly together. You lean on me and keep your eyes closed. I will see for us both.' Step by step, taking her whole weight on himself, and moving forward cautiously, he got her to the edge of the roof. 'Now,' he said. 'You sit down. I shall still hold on to you but I shall slip off.' He quickly slithered down on to the balcony. 'So now you must turn sideways and lower yourself to me. It is not very far. Good, that's right. There you are.' He gripped Jenny firmly and got her down so that she was facing in to the wall. 'Now only ten little steps and we are there.'

Jenny stood as if frozen. 'I can't move,' she said in a small voice. 'I can't—it'll give way . . .'

'It is very easy,' said Tony reassuringly. 'You keep your face to the wall, Jenny, and I shall do the same. Now you see, I am covering you. I take a step and then you take a step . . .' He went on talking, urging, coaxing and encouraging her until she began to move. 'Good. Now stretch out your hand, Jenny. You will feel the door. Good. That's right. There, you are safe. You see, as I tell my team, we have to work together. Now wait one moment, I will go down the stairs first so that you can fall on me—and down again—and we are out.'

Jenny pushed her tangled hair out of her eyes. 'Tony, you're marvellous, you're wonderful!' and she threw her arms around him and gave him a kiss.

Tony drew back as if he'd been struck by an adder. 'No,' he said in a shocked voice, 'it will spoil my training,' and looked very surprised when Jenny laughed rather shakily. For the first time he took a proper look at her. 'You are very dirty,' he said disapprovingly. 'You have blood on your hair. You must try not to be locked in again.'

'I'll try,' said Jenny gravely. As he began to bounce up and down rather impatiently on the balls of his feet, she grabbed hold of his hand. 'Oh no,' she said. 'No more training. Not tonight, Tony. Come on, we've got to find Mike and Mario.'

'But . . .'

Jenny gripped him even more tightly. 'Let's go,' she said and tried to run down the hill. She was so stiff and sore that she could only manage a few steps at a time and she found herself leaning more and more heavily on him.

The sky had become dark purple and the round
yellow moon shone palely in it. It must be getting late,
Jenny thought, and tried to hurry a little faster. As
they went round the last bend and into the centre of
Victoria they were faced with a blaze of lights and an
explosion of sound. Everything was illuminated, everyone was there. Ruthlessly dragging a reluctant Tony
behind her, Jenny elbowed her way through and
made for the widest bit of the road. She pushed and
shoved and squeezed her way through every gap and
where there wasn't one she made one, regardless of
the strange looks that followed her progress. Someone
put his hand up in an official sort of way to stop her
crossing but she blundered past him and reached the
other side just as one of the bands swung round the
corner and spread out over the whole street. 'Tony!'
She had to shriek at the top of her voice to be heard
above the uproar. 'Find out what's happened to the
statue of Our Lady.'

'What?' A file of drummers and trumpeters burst
into a crescendo of sound.

She put her mouth to his ear and shouted again. He
turned to a large man who, with a child on either
shoulder, was jigging up and down in time to the
music. Tony turned back to Jenny. 'They have
already taken her past here,' he said. 'She is now on
her way back to the square. Why?'

Jenny didn't bother to answer him. She jerked at
his hand again and they made their way down a series
of side passages. At least it was less crowded there and
they were able to make better progress. The entrance
into the square was blocked by a large lorry that
practically filled the whole of the alley. One man was
half-heartedly looking into its engine but the driver,
obviously realizing that it made a superb grandstand,
was happily seated on the top of the cab, a glass in his

hand and a bottle by his side, singing loudly and encouraging other people to come up and join him.

Jenny squeezed her way alongside it and came out into the main square at last. It was tightly packed with people already. Jenny's heart sank. How could she hope to find the others in all this? There were thousands of people. It was so jammed that there seemed no room to manoeuvre at all. She could hear the thumping, trampling, tooting and staccato rata-tat-tatting of the band as it approached the square. We'll just have to reach to the steps somehow,' she shouted to Tony. 'At least we'll be able to see if we manage to get up there.'

The façade of the church was brilliantly lit with thousands upon thousands of golden-glowing bulbs; on stands at the far end flaming Catherine wheels twirled round and round, one after another in a kaleidoscope of colour. Jenny had no time to look. Once more she shouldered and pushed and thrust her way through until at last they finally reached the foot of the steps.

'Jenny!' Mario, leaning on the balustrade, grinned down at her. 'Where...?' As she turned to look up at him, his face changed and he ran rapidly down the steps to her. 'What's happened to you? Are you all right? You're cut! Look at those bruises! Jenny!' He put his arm round her and helped her up to the top.

Mike, who had been staring across from the other side, moved over quickly to her side. 'My God!' he exclaimed. 'You look a mess, Jenny. Who did that to you?'

'She locked herself in,' said Tony.

'Locked herself in?' repeated Mike.

'Listen,' said Jenny quickly. 'It's Nick and Al.' She rattled through her story. 'I can hardly believe,' she said at the end of it, 'that I was too dumb to guess what Simon was on about. If I'd had the wit of a flea

I'd have cottoned on to it straight away. What really
beats me is why they only thumped me on the head
and locked me up. They must have known that I'd get
out sooner or later. After all, they won't have had a
chance to get to the statue up to now—you know how
it's always surrounded with people praying and things
just before the festa. They must mean to get it tonight
somehow or other.'

'I still don't see,' said Mike slowly, 'why you weren't
really fixed.'

'What they did know,' said Jenny, is that I can't do
heights. I told them so myself and they must have
known too that the Citadel was going to be deserted.
Maybe they reckoned I wouldn't get out until
morning—and if it hadn't been for Tony, I wouldn't.'

Mike still shook his head. 'There must be something
more to it . . .'

Jenny turned to Mario. 'We must tell the police,'
she said urgently.

'There are no police,' said Mario slowly. 'There has
been a terrible accident off Marselforn. A tanker has
exploded. They are all down there trying to help.'

'Then—' Jenny looked round wildly. 'Someone's in
charge here. There must be someone.'

'Only the marshals from the Band Club,' said
Mario. 'They've taken over. They won't know what
we're talking about. They won't believe us.'

'But they must. They've got to. You've got to make
them.' She stared at Mario and then pushed him.
'You've got to make them understand. Make them turn
the statue upside down. They've only got to look.'

'Jenny, you don't know what you're saying. This
isn't only fun. It's serious. It's religious. They're not
going to stop in the middle of everything and turn it
upside down just on your say-so.'

She nibbled anxiously at her finger-nails. 'But I know they are going to do something,' she said. 'Al and Nick didn't shut me up for nothing.'

'What can they do in front of about five thousand people?' asked Mike.

'How should I know?' she snapped. 'But they will, I know they will.'

While they were talking the main street leading into the centre of the square was slowly being cleared. All the little boys who had been climbing over the wide platform erected along one side of it were being removed. The music was getting louder and louder. Mario suddenly vaulted over the side of the balustrade and dodged over to a man who was forming a chain with some others. He spoke to him urgently. They saw him pouring out words and they saw the man, an incredulous expression on his face, turn away and laugh loudly. Mario went from one to another. They shrugged him off or gave each other meaning looks before turning their backs on him, and finally Mario gave up and returned to them. 'It's just no good,' he said. 'I knew it wouldn't be. They won't listen.'

The leading band marched into the square, red-faced and tired, but still blasting away. Small boys hopped along by their side until they were chased away by the marshals. They stomped right across the empty square and stood marking time, their drums still rolling, until they could hear the strains of the band behind them lilting up the street. Then they thankfully put down their instruments, clambered on to the wooden platform, and gratefully picked up the glasses that people had put there for them.

Mike's arm shot out and he pointed to the left. 'There they are.'

Jenny stood on tiptoe. She could just see the top of Al's sandy head and by jumping she caught a glimpse

of his good-natured freckled face as he turned smil-
ingly to Nick. 'What shall we *do*?' she cried.

'Al and Nick aren't alone,' said Mario soberly.
'They're with at least two other men—and I'm pretty
sure I recognize one of them,' and he rubbed his
stomach thoughtfully.

Tony turned to them, a puzzled look on his face. 'I
do not understand,' he said simply. Mario spoke
swiftly to him and his mouth dropped open. 'No!' he
said at last. 'Is it a joke?'

'No, it's no joke,' said Mario. 'Don't leave. We
might need you.'

A slow and solemn procession began to fill the
square. Ten sweating men, their faces serious, their
footsteps slow, their backs bent under the heavy burden of the statue of Our Lady, her silver and blue
dress glittering under the lights, moved reverently
across the open space. The swelling sound of a hymn
followed them and hundreds of people, their fingers
clutching rosaries, followed closely behind.

Jenny caught a glimpse of Nick's alert face as he
turned and spoke quickly to his companions. 'It'll
happen soon,' she said nervously. 'Let's get down
there.' She darted down the steps and the others rushed
after her.

The noise became indescribable. The second band,
playing a lively tune, had neared the entrance to the
square, while the hymn of those in front was just
reaching its climax. There didn't appear to be even a
square inch of extra room yet more and more people
packed in at every moment so that they were standing
shoulder to shoulder, small children being carried and
lifted high above the crush.

As the strains of the second band died away yet
more petards were exploded, their thunderous cracks
echoing and re-echoing across the sky while at the

same moment dozens of fireworks zoomed up, crackled and burst, so that their brilliant sparks rained down towards the upturned faces. The original band, now refreshed, picked up their instruments once again and began to play an odd tune, lively and catchy, but at the same time sounding strangely religious. Thousands of voices began to sing as the statue itself was transferred to a primitive sort of escalator and slowly, inch by inch, it began to move majestically upwards towards the top of the plinth.

'Let's get closer,' muttered Mario as he caught sight of Nick working his way through the crowd. Long before they got anywhere near it and just as the song died away, the square was emptied. Marshals urged and coaxed the crowds back to the walls so that they overflowed into the side-streets and narrow alleys. Both bands struck up together and the dancing began. Arms were linked, friendly hands groped for others, happy smiles were exchanged, faces lit up and they all began skipping backwards and forwards in two long chains, advancing and retreating and advancing again.

Jenny, one hand grasped by the rough hand of a farm worker, the other tightly gripped by a little boy, danced automatically, in and out and round and round. Suddenly, as the chains swung together once more, she found herself face to face with Nick. 'Jenny!' he cried pleasantly. 'I didn't think you'd make it,' but before she could say a word, they were swept apart again and she found herself with the little boy, galloping madly down a long line of clapping people.

The affair took on a dreamlike quality. She skipped past Mario who was being tightly clasped by a pink satin and lace lady, and lost him again. She was whirled away by an exquisite young man, all black velvet and gold chains, and found herself dancing in a mad kind of foursome reel with Arthur, Edward Albion and Robert. Robert's legs were kicking wildly in the air as he was pushed into the centre and performed a strange kind of solo, an astonished expression on his face the whole of the time, as if he didn't quite know what he was doing there. She was swept away by a beaming soldier and she linked arms with Al, whose laughing face looked down as he said, 'I thought we'd fixed you, you little bitch,' before being dragged into a long chain of women who swayed in and out of a line of men. Someone spun her out of the chain and she found herself alone for a minute.

Pushing her limp hair out of her eyes, she suddenly saw the tall grave figure of Joe staring thoughtfully out over the crowd. She struggled to meet him but a huge hairy arm grasped her and, as she was lifted high into the air and spun round while people laughed and clapped, she saw Joe disappearing down a side-street. Dizzily she looked around. Mike and Mario were steadily making their way closer to the statue but so were Nick and Al. 'Put me down!' she shouted and the giant lowered her gently to the ground. Dazed, she found someone to lean against while she tried to recover herself.

The pattern of the dance changed. Formality had gone. People were prancing about and capering around with anyone who happened to be near. Serious old ladies, their skirts lifted modestly an inch or two above the knee, performed intricate steps, while young children skipped and screamed and ran around. Others, their faces serious and absorbed, danced on their own until someone linked up with them and they were swept away. And then the music ceased abruptly.

People stopped what they were doing. They turned

to the statue once more and began to sing, their voices charged with emotion. There was a jerk, Our Lady shuddered and then began the rest of her journey to the top of the plinth again. Jenny squeezed her way to the front. She saw Al immediately. He looked at his watch and nodded to Nick and the other men.

'Watch out!' she screamed—and the square went black. Every light went out. The brilliant façade of the church disappeared. The street lights flickered and died. The strings of fairy lights in the trees flashed erratically and were extinguished. Only the faint glare of a distant Catherine Wheel as it whirred round and round on its own gave a fading glimmer.

There was a moment of silence and then people shouted. One or two screamed. There was a roar of laughter from somewhere and some nervous giggling. People began striking matches and flicking lighters and little pinpoints of light glimmered in the dark. Suddenly brilliant headlights shone out from the stranded lorry and their beam cut right across the square. Al was bathed in light, one foot on the lower part of the plinth, the other reaching for the ground. The silver-coloured parcel glittered and shone.

'Get him!' roared Mario.

Al tossed the parcel to Nick and stood there coolly for just one second. Mike, charging towards him, halted indecisively, uncertain whether to go for the bundle or for Al and in that fatal moment Al leapt down safely and disappeared. Mario, who made for Nick, was tripped up by someone and he lay gasping for breath for a moment before getting up again and joining in the chase. Tony pounded after Nick, who slipped through a gap in the crowd. But as the people turned, seeming stupefied by the events taking place under their noses, they blocked his path and he hit out wildly in his efforts to get through. Jenny flew after

Mike and eventually they all managed to squirm to the edge of the square. Not one of the men was visible. It was as if they had never been there at all.

'Which way?' asked Mike.

They stood there, straining their ears. Mario caught the dying sound of distant footsteps. 'Through the alley!'' he shouted, and they all turned and raced down the narrow passage and reached the main road just as Nick and Al hurled themselves into their car and took off for Xlendi.

'Well, that's that!' said Jenny bitterly as the tail light disappeared round the corner.

Mario pounded down the road towards his van and then slithered to a halt. Cars were parked all round it. He'd never be able to get it out. 'I guess you're right,' he muttered. 'That really is that.'

'Watch out!' Mike pushed him out of the way as a large Fiat rushed towards them and screeched to a halt. Caldena opened the doors. 'Get in,' he said briefly and began moving again almost before they had all scrambled in. He raced through the narrow streets, cutting corners wherever he dared.

Jenny glanced at his stern face. 'Can you catch them?' Caldena didn't answer but, as he screamed round a corner, he put his foot down even harder. Once they were on the straight they could see the rear lights of the car in front once again. Jenny clutched her seat. 'We're getting closer!' she shrieked as they bounced over the bridge.

Long before they reached the bay they could clearly hear the familiar sound of a boat. Caldena hurtled down the last stretch and then jammed on the brakes. On the far side of the bay, outlined against the phosphorescent sea, they could see a familiar launch and the dim figures of two men stumbling over the rocks and being helped aboard.

They clambered out and stood in a line on the sea-wall. As the boat circled the bay and made for the open sea, glittering rays of light shot out from the sides of the cliffs and danced on the water, forming a silvery web in which the launch buzzed and whined and twisted and turned in a vain attempt to shake them off. From the very top of the cliff-face the beam of a powerful spotlight poured down, bathing the launch in radiant light, as if on a stage. Jenny put her hand to her face and Mike and Mario stared in disbelief and then moved protectively towards her.

More and more lights flickered over the waves as luzzu after luzzu switched on and their golden glow brought yet more illumination to the scene. From far out at sea two powerful craft began to close in, their searchlights sweeping across the water and then holding the launch steadily in their powerful glare. The trapped boat cut its engine. A familiar figure rose and stood silhouetted on the deck, his shaggy greyish-brown hair falling round his face. He held his hands high above his head. A silver packet soared up into the air and then fell silently into the water.

'Oh, James!' said Jenny, her voice shaking. From the shadows Sue appeared. She put her arm round Jenny and led her away.